ONE NIGHT FOR SEDUCTION

ERICA RIDLEY

ISBN: 1943794294
ISBN-13: 978-1943794294

ALSO BY ERICA RIDLEY

***Rogues to Riches*:**

Lord of Chance

Lord of Pleasure

Lord of Night

Lord of Temptation

Lord of Secrets

Lord of Vice

The *Dukes of War*:

The Viscount's Tempting Minx

The Earl's Defiant Wallflower

The Captain's Bluestocking Mistress

The Major's Faux Fiancée

The Brigadier's Runaway Bride

The Pirate's Tempting Stowaway

The Duke's Accidental Wife

The *12 Dukes of Christmas*:

Once Upon a Duke

Kiss of a Duke

Wish Upon a Duke

Never Say Duke

Dukes, Actually

The Duke's Bride

The Duke's Embrace

The Duke's Desire

Dawn With a Duke

One Night With a Duke

Ten Days With a Duke

Forever Your Duke

The *Wicked Dukes Club*:

One Night for Seduction by Erica Ridley

One Night of Surrender by Darcy Burke

One Night of Passion by Erica Ridley

One Night of Scandal by Darcy Burke

One Night to Remember by Erica Ridley

One Night of Temptation by Darcy Burke

CHAPTER 1

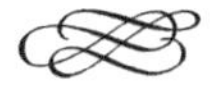

January 22, 1817
London, England

On the afternoon in which Caleb Sutton, fifth Duke of Colehaven, strode into a familiar pub in the heart of the Haymarket district, he did not suspect that his world was on the cusp of being turned upside down… Again.

"Colehaven!" chorused the pub's colorful denizens in unison, raising their mugs in good cheer.

The duke blinked errant snowflakes from his eyelashes and returned their light-hearted grins. Whatever wintry mischief the wind might be making out-of-doors, here inside the tavern known as the Wicked Duke, all was as it should be. Lively conversation, fine ale, friendly faces, and Cole's favorite worn leather seat awaiting him.

He immediately handed off his coat and hat.

"Ten years," Cole said as he took his customary spot between two of his closest friends. "Do you know what this means?"

"We're getting old?" Eastleigh drawled, giving a sardonic arch to his brow.

Valentine Fairfax, sixth Duke of Eastleigh, had not only been Cole's partner in crime since their earliest days at Oxford, but was also fifty percent of the reason they—and, later, their tavern—had earned the moniker *wicked dukes*.

The other fifty percent of the blame lay squarely on Cole's shoulders.

"It means," he continued as he accepted a mug of perfectly frothed ale, "this Season marks the ten-year anniversary of the Wicked Duke tavern. I'd say that's cause for celebration, wouldn't you?"

"I'd say it's cause for a round of drinks on Colehaven!" called a voice from amongst the throng next to the bar.

A sea of glasses clinked in the air as the crowd roared its approval.

"My pockets are to let," Cole protested, affecting a wide-eyed expression. "My sister's millinery expenditures have beggared me. Have you any notion what it costs to clothe a fashionable young lady every Season?"

"Marry her off," Eastleigh suggested.

"If only it were so easy," came a groan from Cole's opposite side, where their friend Thaddeus

Middleton gazed back at them piteously. "If there's a secret maneuver for marrying off unmarriageable ladies, for the love of God, *tell me*."

Cole's voice lowered dangerously. "Did you just call my sister unmarriageable?"

"Felicity could have her pick of husbands by nightfall and you know it," Eastleigh put in. "Middleton's ward is a special case."

"A very special case," Thaddeus agreed. "It cannot be done. You chaps are fortunate that all you have to deal with are your little meetings in the House of Lords. I have a ward who cannot be tamed."

"There's your trouble." Cole sat back. "Your first mistake is believing *any* woman can be tamed. If she suspects that's what you're about, you might as well give up altogether and save yourself the fight."

"I don't know," Thaddeus said doubtfully. "After serving six grueling years at war, you would think I could handle a slip of a girl."

"Girls are far trickier than French soldiers," Eastleigh assured him. "Had we sent a crop of Diamonds of the First Water to the front lines in lieu of the Royal Army, Napoleon would have been trussed up decades ago."

Eastleigh would know. Like Cole, the duke had a sister.

"Tell you what," Cole set down his ale. "When Parliament opens next week, I'll suggest that very thing. All troublesome young ladies who discard suitors like unwanted hairpins will be outfitted with uniforms and muskets and sent to the front lines to train our troops."

"Do not dare him," Eastleigh interrupted before Thaddeus could respond. "You know Colehaven cannot resist a wager. That's half the reason the Wicked Duke exists today."

"I won that bet," Cole pointed out. "We're celebrating the ten-year anniversary of my unbroken winning streak."

"We're celebrating the tenth anniversary of the Wicked Duke," his co-owner corrected. "Besides, I'm not convinced that Vauxhall debacle was anything short of disaster."

"I said I'd *play* the bassoon on center stage," Cole reminded him firmly. "I never said I'd be good at it."

"I dare you," Thaddeus blurted out. At this unintended outburst, a flush immediately colored his cheeks.

Cole wrinkled his nose. "I already did that one."

"Trust me," Eastleigh said with an exaggerated shudder. "If your ears had the misfortune of witnessing him bleat upon a bassoon in front of half of London, you'd agree one such memory is more than enough."

"Not *that*." Thaddeus's dark gaze focused intently on Cole. "I dare you to marry off my unmarriageable ward."

"Fool's errand," Eastleigh scoffed. "If she's unmarriageable, then by definition it cannot be done."

But that old, familiar excitement was already prickling along Cole's skin.

"What makes her unmarriageable?" he asked. It didn't mean he was going to take the wager. It just meant he was... *interested.*

"Her age, for one," Thaddeus admitted. "Even if she wasn't a determined wallflower, most eligible bachelors consider her too long in the tooth for possible consideration."

Cole straightened his spine. Thad's ward was not a shy wallflower or a reluctant wallflower or an accidental wallflower, but rather *determined* to remain one? The lady was becoming more interesting by the minute.

"How many years on the shelf?" he pressed.

Thaddeus sighed. "I'm afraid she's five-and-twenty."

Five-and-twenty. Cole blinked. That ancient age meant the lady was only a scant year older than Cole's younger sister.

His *unwed* younger sister. Who absolutely was still marriageable and was one hundred percent guaranteed to stumble across a suitor too good to turn down.

Someday.

"Five-and-twenty isn't a lost cause," he said quickly. "After all, who wants some chit barely out of the schoolroom? Girls that age are flighty and silly because they haven't experienced enough life yet to build up something worthy to say."

"Ah." Eastleigh stroked his chin in mock

solemnity. "Everyone knows wallflowers are the most experienced at experiencing life."

Cole ignored him.

"There must be something else," he insisted. "Some other reason your ward hasn't found a suitor she's willing to wed."

"The primary reason is that Diana hasn't *had* any suitors." Thaddeus winced. "She may have indicated her intention to refuse any such attention on more than one occasion."

Cole frowned. "If she doesn't wish to wed, what does she intend to do with her life?"

"She enjoys… fixing things," Thaddeus hedged.

"Darning holes in stockings?" Eastleigh guessed from behind his mug of ale. "Mending the occasional rub iron whenever a loose axle nut pops the head block out of alignment on the family barouche?"

"Worse," Thaddeus admitted with a sigh. "Diana arranges other people's lives, whether they want her to or not. She was under my roof for less than a sennight before she'd completely reordered my house, from the ledgers to the rafters. I personally do not mind having my accounts in order, but then she started in on the neighbor—"

"Not the neighbor!" Eastleigh said with a melodramatic gasp.

"—and then the neighbor's neighbor and so on, until I feared a mutiny on my hands. But it wasn't until I caught Diana writing up an earnest, ten-page treatise on how Lady Jersey should better organize her household and her servants, as well as increase the efficiency and quality of Almack's—"

This time, Eastleigh's gasp was unfeigned, and he nearly choked on his beer. "Arrange Lady *Jersey?* Why, if your ward had sent that letter, today she'd be nothing more than a pile of ash and a memory."

Cole's blood fairly danced with anticipation. "A challenge, to be sure."

Eastleigh stared at him. "That's not 'challenging.' That's unmarriageable. This is not a wager you can win."

Cole turned his gaze to Thaddeus. "What are the terms?"

"One hundred pounds," he answered without hesitation. "No, two hundred. If you can make it happen."

"Nobody can make it happen," Eastleigh murmured with a shake of his head. "Lady *Jersey*. Your ward has no sense of self-preservation."

"She has a lot of sense," Thaddeus said staunchly. "Too much sense. She can't look at something without seeing a dozen ways to improve it. Her brain never ceases."

"No wonder you can't marry her off," Eastleigh muttered with a theatrical shiver.

"She'll make some man one hell of a wife," Cole corrected.

Eastleigh arched a brow. "You?"

"Good God, no." Cole reeled backward in horror. He would take a bride eventually—duty to the title, and whatnot—but he was far from ready for a step like that.

Unlike Eastleigh, Cole hadn't been born expecting to inherit a dukedom someday. It had taken years of hard work to learn what others had had a lifetime to discover, and now that he had done so to the best of his ability, he was still fighting to prove himself amongst the peerage. He didn't want to be 'acceptable.' He wanted to excel. To be deemed just as competent as any other blue blood in the House of Lords. And *then* perhaps he'd take a bride.

In the meantime, there was the small matter of an allegedly unmarriageable ward, too preoccupied with arranging others' lives to take care of her own future. Parliament wouldn't be sitting for another week.

What better way to pass the time than by winning a friendly wager?

He turned to Thad. "Not the two hundred quid. I mean what are the terms of the bet? Do I win once she's obtained a serious offer from an interested party, or must we wait until the contract is signed to consider the deed done?"

Thaddeus leaned forward. "You think you can do it?"

"I don't take a wager unless I'm certain of it. I've a ten-year winning streak to consider."

"It's the ale talking," Eastleigh put in.

Cole shoved his mug in the duke's direction. "I've barely touched mine."

"Then it's the lack of ale talking." Eastleigh

pushed the mug back toward Cole. "Finish your beer. Then say 'no.'"

Thaddeus frowned at Eastleigh in confusion. "You don't think he means to do it?"

"Colehaven is rash as a newborn pup, but honest to a fault," Eastleigh said with a sigh. "If he takes a bet, he'll win or die trying. But trust me. Never underestimate a woman."

Ignoring the warning, Thad turned back to Cole, his eyes alive with hope. "Church bells. Suitors are good, a signed contract is better, but not until she's legally someone's wife can the wager be considered won. And there must be a time limit. Shall we say… by the end of the Season?"

Cole inclined his head at this request. Between his sister, his dukedom, and his duties with the House of Lords, Cole wouldn't have a spare moment once the Season got underway. He would wrap up this wager within a week, and then focus on his true responsibilities.

Thad's ward hadn't found a husband because she hadn't been looking for one. How hard could it be to find one for her?

"To keep things fair," Thaddeus added, "no manipulation of the outcome. You can't pay someone to marry her, you can't marry her yourself or pretend to be entranced so that others follow suit. Diana must wed a man she *wishes* to marry, who also wishes to have her for his wife."

"I would never manipulate someone with falsehoods or pretend to be something I am not,"

Cole said stiffly. "If you believe me to be that sort of knave, we needn't wager at all."

"I meant no offense," Thad said quickly. "Diana is not just my ward, but my cousin. I care for her as if she were my sister. You have a sister of your own. I'm trusting you not just to win, but to have a care for Diana's heart."

Eastleigh lifted his beer. "Behind his imprudence and arrogance, Colehaven is a softhearted romantic. If anyone can rustle up a love match for your ward, it's a dreamer like him."

"Five hundred pounds," Thaddeus blurted eagerly. "If that's not enough, name your price."

Cole's brain was already five moves ahead. "Where is your ward right now?"

"Home."

Perfect. Cole's blood sang with excitement. Per the terms of the wager, he couldn't be seen as 'dancing attendance upon her' publicly, but a quick detour to the Middleton town house wouldn't raise any eyebrows. Anyone who glimpsed the family crest upon his carriage would assume Cole to be paying a call to Thaddeus, not his ward.

Who, Cole belatedly realized, was so effective at being a wallflower that he hadn't the least idea what she looked like. He had a vague idea that Thaddeus had become her guardian a year or two earlier, but no memory of ever having formally met her.

Until now.

No time like the present to make her acquaintance, Cole decided. He'd get a sense of Diana Middleton's personality, find out what she wanted in a husband, and work out the particulars tomorrow. Between the beau monde and the Wicked Duke, Cole was friends with half of London. Any number of fine gentlemen should suit. With luck, he'd have the matter sorted before the weekend.

"I accept your terms," he announced and pushed to his feet. Before either of his friends could add more fuel to the fire, Cole hurried toward the door.

Startled, Eastleigh jumped to his feet. "You didn't finish your beer!"

"It's my tavern," Cole said over his shoulder as he shrugged back into his greatcoat and gloves. "I can have ale any time I please."

"You own *half* of the tavern," Eastleigh called after him as Cole strode out the door.

CHAPTER 2

The chilly winter air was just as bracing this time around, but Cole barely registered the wind tugging the brim of his hat or the plumes of snow kicked up by passing horses. He swung himself into his waiting coach and directed his driver to the Middleton town house just outside Mayfair, part of a neatly kept terrace less than a mile from Cole's home on Grosvenor Square.

A faint smile curved his lips as he strode up the front steps to the frozen iron knocker. When the Season was not in session, the thing Cole missed most was the sensation of being *useful*. Every moment in the House of Lords was dedicated to doing good works; to improving the lives of others.

Playing matchmaker to a wallflower did not perhaps compare to his work on the Bank of England Act or the Customs and Excise Act or Sykes' Hydrometer Act, but Cole considered the pursuit of love and happiness as worthy a cause as any other measure.

In fact, he was hoping this exercise with the Middleton lass would prove good practice for when it came time to see his sister happily settled. For all her maddening ways, he loved Felicity dearly and hoped to see his sister in the sort of love match poets would wax lyrical about for centuries to come.

The door opened, revealing the ruddy cheeks of the Middleton family butler.

His eyes widened in recognition. "Your Grace."

There was no need to present a calling card. Cole and Thaddeus had been firm friends ever since the Wicked Duke first opened its doors a decade ago. Although most of their meetings took place at the tavern, they had visited each other's homes on occasion. It was always a pleasure.

"How do you do, Shaw?"

Cole was fairly certain dukes were not *meant* to greet other peoples' servants by name, but as he had spent more than half his life without the slightest indication he would someday inherit a title—much less a dukedom—this simple kindness was a long-ingrained habit he had no intention of breaking.

"Very well, Your Grace, thank you." Shaw did not move aside. "I'm afraid Mr. Middleton is not at home."

"As it happens, I have not come to call upon Thaddeus," Cole answered with a smile. "Is Miss Middleton receiving callers?"

"I..." Shaw stumbled backward as if the request had quite literally bowled him over. "This call is for... *Miss* Middleton, Your Grace?"

Cole did his best to keep his smile in place, despite the tiny worm of doubt now wriggling in his stomach. He understood the young lady was considered a wallflower; understood that to date there had been no interested gentlemen, but Shaw's unfeigned shock at such a simple request could lead a man to think Miss Middleton had never received a single caller at all.

Nonsense, Cole assured himself. "Wallflower" was not synonymous with "invisible." Surely the lady had *some* friends.

"Just so," he said firmly. "I've come to call on Miss Middleton. Is the lady at home?"

"I..." Shaw's hands fluttered like trapped birds. The bafflement on the butler's face only grew more pronounced. "Do come in out of the cold. You're familiar with the guest parlor. Please warm yourself by the fire while I check to see if... Miss Middleton is... receiving callers."

It wasn't until Cole stood before the front salon's familiar crackling fire that he realized he was still wearing his coat and gloves, as if Shaw took it as a matter of course that even if Miss Middleton *was* at home, she would not be receiving callers.

Even a duke.

Movement caught the corner of Cole's eye and he turned to see a maid slip into the salon. Possibly sent to offer him some sort of refreshment as he waited but, given how the mission was unfolding thus far, more likely the girl was simply going about her normal routine. Shaw would return at any moment to inform Cole his mistress had no wish to make his acquaintance.

He gave a subtle nod to acknowledge the maid's presence and moved out of her way to sit upon the edge of a sofa.

The maid tilted her head as if considering him, but the brim of her mobcap flopped too low for Cole to discern the direction of her gaze. Of course a servant wouldn't be so ill-trained as to stare rudely at her master's guests. Likely she was deciding between carrying on with her duties or returning later once the unexpected guest had gone.

"You're one of Diana's friends?" came the soft query.

Cole wasn't certain what startled him more: confirmation that Diana Middleton did indeed have friends, or surprise that a maid would dare to address him directly.

Perhaps that was why his mouth answered automatically, "I'm here to see Miss Middleton, yes."

Even that small evasion caused a ripple of discomfort beneath his skin. It was none of the maid's business what the Duke of Colehaven was or was not up to, but Cole prided himself on being scrupulously honest in all his dealings, regardless of situation or class. Yet he could not bring himself to say *No, I am not her friend* aloud. Honesty was paramount, but so was honor, and he was not here to besmirch Miss Middleton's.

"Is she expecting you?" the maid asked.

"She is not," he replied tightly, and made a show of arranging his long limbs in the opposite direction as though he had become struck with sudden fascination at the wallpaper on the other side of the parlor.

There. That should put paid to further inquiries.

"Then why are you here?" the maid insisted. "Have you come to press a suit?"

"*Nothing* like that," Cole blurted out more forcefully than he intended. He gave up on the far wallpaper and turned to glare at the impertinent maid in the doorway.

She was no longer in the doorway. The maid now stood an arm's length from the other side of the sofa. Her enormous mobcap still flopped too low for her eyes to be visible, but her slender fingers worried at each other against the starched panel of her apron.

The chit *ought* to be worried. If one of the Middletons caught her interrogating a guest… Or if the head housekeeper should spy her underling shirking her duty…

"Haven't you anything to do?" Cole said at last. He was not rude by nature, but then again, he normally did not find himself in conversation with other peoples' chambermaids. Reminding her of her duty was doing her a favor, he told himself. If she lost her post due to such antics, Cole would not be to blame.

"I have more to do than time to do it," the maid said.

Cole did not doubt this. He gestured toward the opposite side of the parlor. "Don't let me stop you from what you came to do."

To his surprise, her lithe hands retrieved a small journal from the pocket of her apron, jotted a quick note with the nub of a pencil, and tucked both objects back inside as though they'd never existed.

"Where's your chaperone?"

"*I* don't require a chaperone. It's Miss Middleton who—" He broke off as a sudden thought occurred to him, unlikely as it might seem. "Are *you* the young lady's chaperone? Have you come to assess my character?"

"Did you hope for a stolen moment alone with her?" the maid countered.

"Heaven forbid." He could not repress a shiver of horror. "I would never be caught alone with a marriageable young lady."

"You've no wish to marry?"

"None," he replied firmly. And definitely no wish to be compromised against his will.

"Then what makes you think Miss Middleton has any intention to marry?"

"Of course she intends to marry," Cole said in exasperation. "All proper young ladies hope to find a worthy husband and become an equally worthy wife. What else is she going to do?"

"Mathematics," the maid replied without hesitation.

He blinked at this non sequitur. "What sort of woman prefers mathematics to marriage?"

"A wise one," the maid snapped. She ripped off her mobcap and glared at him, revealing a beautiful pair of angry blue eyes. "I'd rather devote the rest of my life to applied sums and long division than spend a single second in the presence of yet another man who thinks he knows what a woman wants without bothering to perform the most perfunctory of information gathering interviews to determine—"

"Miss Middleton?" stammered from his mouth, but Cole need not await verbal confirmation to recognize the truth. "Why are you dressed like a maid?"

"Why are you alone with me in this parlor?" she countered, hands on her hips.

At this unfortunate moment, Cole noticed that when the "maid" entered the salon, she'd shut the door behind her. His stomach bottomed in abject fear. If she hadn't known he was coming, why on earth was she wearing a disguise? *Had* she known he was coming?

"Please tell me this was not an elaborate trick to compromise me into marriage," he managed, every muscle tensing in anticipation of the worst.

"No," Miss Middleton said, blue eyes flashing, "it is *leverage* which I intend to use to force you to leave me *alone*."

"You mean to extort a *duke*?" He paused as full realization set in. "Into *not* marrying you?"

"Is it working?" she demanded.

He rose to his feet with alacrity. "I harbor no wish to marry you. None. At all."

"Splendid," she said. "Now hear this. I don't need you or any man. Understood? If you've any sense of self-preservation, you'll find your way out of this town house before someone catches us alone together and both our lives are ruined."

God help them both.

He dashed to the door and flung it open wide, to prove no nefarious seduction was underway in the guest parlor. But Miss Middleton was right. Lack of misdeed would not be enough. He needed to make haste before the distinct lack of chaperonage in the parlor forced them into an unwanted marriage.

Sensing any act of politeness would only serve to irritate her further, Cole tipped his hat as he swept past her. "Pleasure to make your acquaintance, Miss Middleton. Have a lovely day."

"I'm already delighted never to have to see you again," she called after him, her plump lips pursed in victory.

He smiled to himself as he returned to his carriage.

That was where the fiery Miss Middleton was wrong. They would definitely be seeing each other again. After all, he had a ten-year winning streak to protect.

And the Duke of Colehaven *never* backed down from a dare.

CHAPTER 3

Miss Diana Middleton tried her darnedest to focus her attention on the proper calibration of the wine merchant's measurement tools, but her mind kept wandering to yesterday's unexpected visitor. It was not the first time the Duke of Colehaven had deigned to cross their humble threshold, but it was unquestionably the first time any such gentleman had asked to call upon Diana.

"Is it right?" came the querulous voice of the wine peddler. "May I return to selling my wares?"

Diana could not be fooled by feigned innocuousness. This was not the first time she'd been forced to give similar establishments a stern warning.

"You know as well as I do that the weight of a proper wine gallon is never measured against a half-peck ale gallon, but rather a half-peck corn gallon whilst filled with wheat," she scolded him.

His rheumy gaze turned crafty. "How am I supposed to remember something like that?"

"Write it down," she said firmly. She slipped her hand into the basket dangling from her arm and handed him one of the many pre-made reminders she'd drawn out the night before. "Don't lose it this time."

He sighed as he accepted the card with its precisely drawn diagrams. "Yes, Mrs. Peabody."

Diana was not, of course, Mrs. Peabody. Mrs. Peabody did not exist.

Nonetheless, many shopkeepers in this corner of London believed Mrs. Peabody to be a frazzled and woefully underpaid "inspections secretary" to a ruthless barrister, and whose continued employment depended upon her reporting back to her litigious master as many cases of flagrant disregard to the 1815 Weights and Measures Act as she could uncover, so that all such miscreants might be brought to justice.

Due to an arrangement Diana had made with a barrister's assistant, however, any inquiries referencing Mrs. Peabody or a "weights and measures inspections secretary" were forwarded to an anonymous account only Diana had access to. Her credentials were rarely questioned—merchants engaging in illegal conduct wished to call *less* attention to themselves, not *more*—making the indomitable "Mrs. Peabody" quite powerful indeed.

"If I find your tools overcharging customers again…" she said in warning.

"I know, I know." The shopkeeper hurried to

tack the reminder card to the wall above the weighing station. "If there's a next time, I shall be defending myself not to a pip of a girl, but to a judge capable of doing far worse than simply dismantling my business."

Diana gave a sharp nod of approval. She did not mind being referred to as a pip of any type as long as it meant future clients to this establishment were no longer at risk of being defrauded. It was often far easier to frighten unscrupulous owners into compliance than it was to convince the courts to pay any mind to the dozens of anonymous complaints she'd submitted to the "proper channels" this winter alone.

She took her leave from the shopkeeper and made her way back out onto the snow-dusted streets of the Haymarket.

It was far too early in the morning for any self-respecting member of the ton to be out of bed, but all the same Diana was clad in one of her many disguises.

Like most of her ensembles, today's was designed to attract the least amount of attention possible. A serviceable gray day gown enshrouded by an even duller gray ankle-length pelisse and a thick woolen shawl. Hair tucked beneath a sturdy but colorless bonnet, whose extensive brim ensured both a respectable distance from passers-by and sufficient shadow to blur her face.

Woolen stockings, no-nonsense black boots, and a thick basket all contributed to the impression of a woman on a mission, like any number of the other servants dashing hither and yon on shopping trips for their masters.

"Inconsequential errand girl" was second only to "chambermaid" in its effectiveness at rendering her positively invisible to members of the upper classes. Nonetheless, in addition to her trusty journal and the weights and measures reminder cards, Diana's basket also contained a scarlet redingote and festive bonnet, should she need to dash behind a folding screen in order to emerge a completely different person.

A hurried change of clothes next to some shopkeeper's chamber pot had thus far never proved necessary. Diana hoped her run of good fortune would last for many more years—until monitoring unethical business practices was no longer necessary or until women could openly helm such a career without raising eyebrows, whichever came first.

She bit back a sigh. Neither outcome was likely to occur in her lifetime. In the best of scenarios, she would be eighty years old, disguised as the elderly mother of some litigious barrister, who had nothing better to do with her time than inspect the measurement tools of London shops in order to report her findings back to her dear son.

Maybe not a litigious barrister, Diana decided. If she was still doing this fifty years from now, she'd claim her grandson was a well-connected justice of the court. What polite soul hoping to keep his shop would dare to argue with a grandmother?

Diana indulged a quick grin at the image. It always tickled her to think of herself as a secret agent to the Crown. So secret, even the Crown itself did not realize she labored in its name. Just a humble sleuth, avenging misapplied mathematics every day for the betterment and fair treatment of all England's citizens.

She slid her journal from the basket and added a quick entry describing the encounter with the wine distributor. When she finished, she flipped to a bookmarked page where she left notes of which establishments required a return visit to ensure honest business dealings were being upheld.

Her threat had not been idle. If the shopkeeper resumed dishonest business practices, she would use every bit of her limited power to see him brought to justice.

She closed the journal. The cover read, *If something can be improved, improve it.* Diana had penned the phrase herself. It had been her motto for as long as she could remember and her secret vocation ever since she'd become the ward of her cousin Thaddeus.

At first, she'd simply needed something to fill her year of mourning besides staring at empty walls or sobbing into her pillows. *Doing* instead of just *dreaming* had given her something to live for. A purpose. A small spot of brightness to fill her otherwise bleak days. And a chance to be someone other than a penniless orphan for an hour or two. An opportunity to be… *important.* To make a difference in people's lives.

She narrowed her eyes down the snow-covered lane. On the other side of the Theatre Royal stood a far less opulent establishment known as the Wicked Duke.

Although women were allowed in the tavern, Diana had never ventured inside. Partly because to enter the front door as herself would ruin any hope of maintaining the level of reputation required to be accepted amongst the ton. Diana did not seek a high-in-the-instep suitor, but nor did she seek to bring public embarrassment to the cousin whose charity had given her a second chance at life.

The other reason was *also* Thad. No amount of billowing woolen shawl or floppy-brimmed bonnet would prevent her own flesh and blood from seeing through her disguise, if he got a good look at her close up.

Not that Thad was there at the moment. He was at home, expecting to take a meal with Diana in less than an hour. Forty-five minutes was not nearly enough time to spy on the Wicked Duke and return home while the food was hot. She bit her lip.

Ignorance of the Wicked Duke's goings-on had never bothered her before. It was a public tavern and for all purposes Thad's "club," seeing as he lacked the title or the connections to be welcomed into a proper club like White's or Boodle's or Brooks's.

The Wicked Duke's clientele ranged from the working class to political reformers to indolent poets and infamous bluestockings. Yet the owners were the highest peers of the realm, giving the fashionable-adjacent establishment an air of pomp and legitimacy, attracting second sons and titled bachelors alike. The sort of self-important men Diana had long hoped never to be trapped in conversation with. Whatever antics unfolded within the Wicked Duke's walls had never piqued her interest.

Until now.

"Don't do it," she muttered to her twitching boots. "Do not head in that direction."

The only reason she was even thinking about the Wicked Duke was because she'd chased one of its namesakes from her front parlor.

Maddeningly, the Duke of Colehaven was not what she had anticipated at all.

Diana *prided* herself on her ability to think ten steps ahead of everyone else. If life was a game of chess, she wasn't a mere player but rather the craftsman designing the game.

The impeccable attention to appearances? Yes, she'd expected that much. Champagne-shined Hessians, buttery soft buckskins, coal black greatcoat, intricately tied neckcloth, closely shorn jaw, dazzling hazel eyes, ridiculously handsome. She'd seen an illustration of His Grace once in a caricature. The artist had got the duke's unceasing perfection right, but failed to convey the most unnerving aspect of Colehaven's character.

The confounding man was *nice*.

Because Diana had been on her way out for one of her reconnaissance missions, she'd reached the ground floor just in time to overhear the duke greet the butler warmly and by name.

Then, when confined in a parlor with an increasingly insolent housemaid, the duke had unflaggingly continued to treat her like a person and respond to her queries, rather than dismiss her out of hand as a servant beneath his notice.

Inconceivable. And yet it had happened.

Extorting him into a hasty retreat had been a calculated risk. He clearly knew nothing of Diana Middleton, but Diana made it her business to know as much as possible about him. She had an entire journal dedicated to the most important members of the ton. The depth and richness of its contents made *Debrett's Peerage* look like a lazy extract.

Caleb Sutton, fifth Duke of Colehaven. Hair, black. Eyes, hazel. Birthdate, the twentieth of August, 1787. Two years to the day before Jurij Vega—one of Diana's mathematical heroes—calculated pi to the 140th place, correcting a computation error made by Thomas Fantet de Lawny almost seventy years earlier. *If something can be improved, improve it.* Vega was a man after Diana's own heart. Why, his 1794 comprehensive thesaurus on logarithms—

Diana shook her head. She was analyzing the

Duke of Colehaven, not continental mathematicians.

Like many eligible bachelors bearing both title and coin, Colehaven had quite a reputation. Unlike most of his peers, Colehaven's reputation was neither that of shameless rake or an arrogant prig, but rather of a well-respected, unflaggingly honest, genuinely nice human, whose greatest vices appeared to be a talent for brewing fine ale, open friendliness toward lower classes, and a penchant for accepting silly dares.

That must be what he was doing in her parlor. One of his cronies must have dared him to pay a call on the most uncelebrated wallflower in London. There. Call paid. End of association. They'd crossed paths once in twenty-five years. With luck, another quarter century would pass before they crossed paths again.

After all, Diana did her level best to stay clear of his world. She didn't want to waltz, didn't want to flirt behind painted fans, and definitely didn't want a husband. The only way her good works could continue was if she remained in charge of her own life.

Resolute, she turned her back toward the Wicked Duke and caught the first hackney back to Jermyn Street, where she slipped in the terrace's rear entrance, deposited her basket and outerwear in her bedchamber, and made it downstairs to the family dining room five minutes before her cousin.

Their great-aunt Ruthmere had moved in

when Thaddeus became Diana's guardian, but due to her age and health, now rarely ventured from her private quarters. Diana brought her fresh books once a fortnight from a traveling library, and knew better than to expect her great-aunt to be awake at such an early hour.

Her cousin entered the dining room with his dark hair unkempt and a guilty smile, as if he'd rolled out of bed a scant moment earlier.

Diana returned Thad's smile with warmth. He was more like a brother than a guardian. Plus, the fact that her family were slugabeds was a boon. By the time they exchanged greetings each day, her true work was already done.

"Chess tonight?" he asked.

She arched a brow. "Aren't you tired of losing?"

He shrugged and reached for the platter of fruit and cheese. "I'll get you someday."

Diana doubted it, but very much appreciated the effort. She and her father had often played chess deep into the night. She still felt the loss of those precious moments keenly, but it was a little better now that she had Thaddeus.

Ever since the day he'd caught her playing a lackluster chess game against herself, he'd immediately offered himself as her partner.

Although not as skilled a player as her father—a man whom Diana had only managed to best on three exceedingly rare occasions—Thad was upbeat and cheerful, keeping up a steady one-sided conversation of on-dits and jests until Diana's sorrow faded to the background and she began to enjoy life again. She owed Thad for that. He was not just a cousin, but a friend. Her dearest and *only* friend.

Which made his next words all the more shocking.

"I think you should take advantage this Season and find a husband." He winked at her. "You're not getting any younger."

Diana's fork clattered against her plate.

"You're not getting younger, either," she spluttered. "Why don't you find a wife?"

"I intend to," he said with a shrug. "Eventually. Fortunately for me, unwed gentlemen of two-and-thirty are not labeled 'spinsters' but rather 'a fine catch.'"

"You're a terrible catch," she grumbled. "No matter how many times I tell you not to lead with F4, you insist upon opening yourself up to a two-move checkmate."

"I have no idea what you're saying," he said cheerfully as he served himself a healthy portion of meat. "F4, 2B, 86, XD. It sounds like a military cipher you've intercepted from some foreign shore."

"I wish I *could* join the military," she muttered. "I would make a splendid secret agent for the Crown."

"Eat your vegetables," Thad advised her. "And don't make such scandalous claims in polite company, or you'll never have a suitor."

Exactly the plan.

CHAPTER 4

"Finally." Cole leaned forward off the squab and reached for the carriage door.

"Stop that," Felicity scolded with a devilish twinkle in her eyes. "Younger sisters are supposed to drag their elder brothers to these things, not the other way around."

"It's the first major rout of the Season," Cole protested, moving his fingers closer to the door handle. "Everyone will be there. Including us!"

With a laugh, Felicity knocked his hand from the door. "At least wait for the coach to stop before you leap out to catch up with four hundred and one of your closest friends."

"Four hundred and twelve," he corrected solemnly. "I've been busy since breakfast."

Cole's propensity to befriend everyone he met was a long-running family jest based firmly in reality. For him, the greatest advantage to owning a tavern was not the unlimited supply of fresh-brewed ale, but the equally unlimited stream of old friends and new faces.

He felt much the same about Society gatherings. Any fête that styled itself "the crush of the Season" meant he was bound to bump into bosom friends he hadn't seen since last Season, old schoolmates he hadn't seen since Oxford, as well as a new crop of strangers a mere introduction away from becoming casual acquaintances or possibly even friends.

When the tiger swung open the door to hand Felicity from the coach, Cole all but bounded out on her heels.

In moments, the butler greeted them at the door, their winter outerwear was spirited away by industrious footmen, and he and his sister stood at the head of a beautiful staircase. Sparkling glass chandeliers illuminated the sprawling ballroom beneath.

Fashionable gentlemen, elegant ladies, sumptuous refreshments, an extravagant orchestra… Cole could scarcely wait for their names to be announced so that he and his sister could join the fun.

"His Grace, the Duke of Colehaven, and Lady Felicity Sutton."

At last! Cole grinned at his sister and held out his arm to escort her into the grand milieu.

Part of the reason Cole befriended everyone he met was because some gentleman out there was the right one for Felicity… and she showed no signs of hunting him down herself.

His sister was no wallflower—Felicity had several close friends and no shortage of names on her dance card—but if the Season were to abruptly end the day after tomorrow, she would not weep at the loss. She was just as content milling in some poet's drawing room or losing an entire afternoon in a library as she was standing up for a waltz with an earl.

"Don't meddle," she said as if she could read his mind. "I will dance if I want to, and it's no business of yours."

"I'm *supposed* to meddle," he reminded her cheerfully. "'God-given right to meddle' came with the title. I participate in making laws that govern all of England. Perhaps the next will be called The Great Felicity Sutton Betrothal Act of 1817."

"God help us all," Felicity muttered, but she could not repress a fond smile. "What year will The Great Duchess of Colehaven Act take place?"

"*Shh,*" he whispered urgently. "Don't make such jests with matchmaking mamas within earshot. I'll be beset by so many fresh-faced debutantes, I won't even be able to move my arms."

"That only happened once," she scolded him, then thought it over.

"Twice," they said in unison.

"The Lyndon soirée," she agreed with a wry shake of her head. "I thought they were going to leap upon you like kittens. You could've taken the whole pack home, if you'd wanted."

He shuddered. "I did not want."

There would eventually be a Duchess of Colehaven, but she would *not* be some giggly seventeen-year-old chit fresh out of the schoolroom. The future Her Grace would be a decorous, intelligent woman, beloved and respected by their peers. A friendly, dignified lady with impeccable manners and a sweet soul, capable of commanding her household and her husband's heart with the crook of her finger. A proper duchess by any measure.

Cole was not at all ready for such a woman. He needed to earn the privilege. Become a respected peer not just in title, but in truth. Perhaps once he'd been chosen to lead a committee, once it was finally *his* ideas changing the world for the better—

"Is there a library somewhere?" Felicity asked.

"Don't you dare." He trapped her hand about his elbow and dragged her in the direction of the orchestra. "No books until you've stood for at least five sets. And try the cakes. If you don't try the lemon drizzle cakes because you're hiding in the library, I'll eat every last tasty morsel, and then you'll be sad."

"You're the worst brother. The very worst. You know lemon tarts are my weakness."

The one thing she liked more than libraries, in fact. Both of which were Cole's fault.

When they were poor, fine confections were the one treat he scrimped and saved for twice a year. Felicity's birthday, and Christmas Eve. With the tart, delicious sweetness melting in their mouths, they could forget the weight of poverty for a moment and enjoy a small slice of heaven.

The title had brought a tidal wave of money and privilege. Suddenly Cole was off to Oxford and no longer needed to sweep chimneys in order to spoil his sister with a sugary treat.

After sharing every joy and despair of their lives together, it hadn't been fair for only Cole to gain the advantage of higher education. He couldn't send his sister to Eton, but there was no reason for her to be ignorant. He sent home every book he could find that could improve her mind or provide an hour's entertainment. Every day after lessons, he penned long letters summarizing the key points of everything he'd learned.

Although many long miles separated them, it was as though they attended Oxford together. From the day Felicity had held her first book in her hands, her love affair with libraries had grown unabated.

"Five sets," he reminded her. "Find five gentlemen worthy of half an hour of your time, and I will escort you to the closest stack of books with a plate of lemon tarts in each hand."

"Very well." The sparkle in her eyes belied her sulky pout. "If these paragons of dandihood bore me to tears, I may send you back to the refreshment table for a second round of fortifications."

"Fair enough." He grinned to himself as his sister melted into the crowd.

Knowing Felicity, she would dance until her feet could not bear another reel. And then, after six or eight or ten whirlwind sets, she would absolutely seek refuge amongst the closest towers of books and not emerge until the coach was ready to take her home.

"There you are," came a voice from behind Cole's shoulder.

He turned to grin at his friend, the Duke of Eastleigh. "Oversleep from last night?"

"Wrap up the Middleton betrothal yet?" Eastleigh countered.

"I will," Cole assured him.

"No hauling her out to the dance floor so that the young bucks copy you," Eastleigh reminded him. "And no marrying her yourself."

Cole rolled his eyes toward the arched ceiling. "I remember the rules."

Indeed, the rules were the least of his concerns. The next time he crossed paths with the unpredictable Miss Middleton, she was just as likely to toss a cup of ratafia in his face as she was to rip off a painted mask and reveal herself to be an articulate kangaroo.

"You would remember," Eastleigh agreed. "I've never seen a man memorize so many obscure particulars as when you were on that Foreign Packets Act committee."

Cole shrugged. "I like committees."

They didn't just make him feel useful. They *were* useful. Importation, exportation, debt reduction, peace preservation, pillory abolition... all those were just in the past year It had been a joy and a privilege to do his part.

"If you like them so much, you should take over for Lord Fortescue."

Worry creased his brow. "Did something happen to the earl?"

"Gravity happened whilst sledding too close to a tree," Eastleigh answered dryly. "He'll be confined to his bed with a fracture-box to keep him company for the next six weeks. When Parliament opens on Tuesday, the first act will be determining someone to replace him in the committees he helmed."

Cole was a member of both the committees Fortescue helmed: Public Works and Fisheries, and Offices of Exchequer. Excitement rushed through his veins.

This was the opportunity he'd been waiting for. If he could convince the Lords to choose him as interim leader, he could prove himself to be as knowledgeable, passionate, and capable as any of the peers that had been born to their roles. Because he'd only been "important" for half his life, Cole had worked twice as hard. He didn't want to be "as good as" any other. He wanted to be exceptional. This would be visible proof that he was worthy of the title he'd inherited.

"You think they'll put it to a vote on Tuesday?"

"I think they'll accept nominations on Tuesday," Eastleigh answered with a shrug. "They probably won't put it to a vote for another week."

Then the clock was set. Cole needed the Middleton dare sorted by Monday evening at the latest. On Tuesday, he would present himself as a serious, dignified contender. Then no more wagers until after he was elected interim committee leader.

No—until after he was designated head of some topic in his own right. Perhaps passenger vessels or night poaching. Cole wasn't picky. He would simply have to mind his Ps and Qs for the next several weeks. Once he threw his hat into the committee leader ring, he could not risk some blunder of comportment preventing him from being considered as an equal.

"If you'll excuse me," Eastleigh murmured. "I believe I've caught sight of the very reason I accepted this invitation."

Under normal circumstances, a statement that suspicious would have piqued Cole's curiosity.

Nothing was normal anymore.

He'd already completely forgotten whatever intrigue the duke might have afoot, because his gaze was now sharpened on a slight bend in the shadows against the far wall of the crowded ballroom. He moved closer, weaving between passing lords and ladies, careful not to give his position away.

Diana Middleton. He was sure of it.

Swathed in a pale rose gown that matched the silk wallpaper so precisely he could almost believe she'd specifically selected the color in order to become a living *trompe l'oeil,* more than capable of fooling the average eye.

What the devil was the chit about? Irritation tickled his skin. He was not fascinated by her,

Cole assured himself. Rosy lips and beautiful blue eyes would not sway him. He believed in honesty and transparency and fairness above all things, and Diana Middleton was nothing but lies and disguises.

She did not appear to be in conversation with anyone else. She was not eating, not drinking, not smiling, not frowning, not blinking so much as an eyelash… Cole wasn't certain whether he should be suspicious or concerned. "Wallflower" was supposed to be a metaphor. Usually due to shyness or plainness or some other so-called flaw that kept unimaginative gentlemen from taking a second look.

This—whatever "this" was—appeared to be by design. Miss Middleton was not seated amongst the spinsters and chaperones, but plastered to the shadows far behind them. Even a gentleman who wandered this far expressly for the purpose of inviting a wilting rose to dance could be forgiven for failing to notice the spitfire doing her best to blend with the wall.

Cole turned before she noticed that he was onto her ruse. Finding her a suitor was not going to be as simple as calculating which gentleman of his acquaintance possessed a personality that best complemented Miss Middleton's. That was no longer step one, but rather step fifteen.

His first act would apparently need to be peeling Thad's ward from the wainscoting. And since he couldn't be seen influencing the wager by paying special attention to her himself… Cole required reinforcements.

When in war, there was no better general to have on one's side than Lady Felicity.

He caught her just as she was sidling toward the refreshment stand.

"A dozen lemon tarts," he murmured as he blocked her path. "I'll bake them personally."

Her brown eyes narrowed. "What did you do?"

"Nothing," he protested as he steered her toward a more private corner. "There's something I need you to do."

She arched her brows. "I'm listening."

He took a deep breath. "Do you know Diana Middleton?"

Felicity blinked. "No."

"Have you heard her name before?"

She frowned in thought, then shook her head. "Why?"

A vision of long-lashed blue eyes and plump, kissable lips filled his head. Cole pushed it away. "I need her to find her true love."

"Is it you?"

"It is not me," he said quickly. "Right now it's nobody, because nobody seems to know she exists."

"Except for you?"

"And her guardian. Thaddeus Middleton."

Felicity nodded slowly. "Thad is a good chap. He should bring his ward to one of these soirées."

"She's *at* one of these soirées." Cole tilted the

back of his head toward the opposite wall. "She's at *this* soirée."

Felicity's brow creased. "What am I looking for? Blond ringlets? Brown chignon? The girl with a feather in her hair?"

"The one whose gown is made out of the same fabric as the wallpaper," he answered grimly. "The one who looks like she might be *part* of the wallpaper."

Almost a full minute passed before Felicity's eyes widened. "I see… something?"

Cole nodded. "It's a small favor. A tiny one. Introduce yourself, then introduce her to… everyone you know. Especially the gentlemen. I'll take it from there."

"This is a dare, isn't it?" Felicity crossed her arms. "Who put you up to this? Was it Eastleigh? Why the deuce am *I* involved?"

"Don't say 'deuce,'" he scolded her. "Wait until you've some hapless fool wrapped about your finger, and then feel free to swear like a sailor."

"Sailors don't say 'deuce,'" she informed him with a flutter of her lashes. "Sailors say 'to the devil with you' and 'I'll be damned if I will' and 'of all the bloody ballrooms in England, you had to stroll into my—'"

He grabbed his sister by the shoulders and spun her toward the spinsters and duennas. "I'll owe you."

Her expression turned crafty. "You'll take me shopping?"

"You have unlimited access to my purse

strings," he reminded her through clenched teeth. "Why do you need *my* presence?"

"Because you hate it," she replied sweetly.

"You tried to outfit me in vermilion stripes and puce muslin," he reminded her. "I'll never forgive you for that. You get lemon tarts or no deal."

"I'm not doing this for you, but for the mystery of it." Felicity narrowed her eyes toward Miss Middleton. "And for the lemon tarts."

CHAPTER 5

"Dance with me."

Diana glanced up to find her cousin Thaddeus sweeping toward her, one dark curl clinging to his temple after several consecutive sets upon the dance floor.

She shook her head. "I'm fine right here. Besides, I think the Everett twins are going to expire on the spot if you don't add your name to their cards."

He hesitated. "You're certain you don't wish to dance?"

"As certain as Adrien-Marie Legendre's prime number theorem," she assured him.

Thaddeus frowned. "Doesn't a theory mean you're *not* certain?"

"A hypothesis means you're not certain, but hoping to find out," she corrected. "Theories, however, are substantiated by evidence. And a theorem—" Diana broke off her recitation and shooed her cousin toward the orchestra. "Go and dance. If you truly wish to know the intricacies of theorems, I'll provide an exhaustive explanation the next time I decimate you at the chess board. For now, Everett twins. Off with you. Shoo."

With a final concerned look, Thaddeus bowed his acquiescence and loped off toward the dance floor.

Diana sagged against the wall in relief.

Although she had never taken him up on his kind offers, Thad never tired of inviting her to join him for a country dance or a minuet. The problem was not Thad, or even minuets. Diana enjoyed the freedom of dancing, and missed it very much.

Just like she missed rakish bonnets with bold peacock feathers and altering her frocks to ape the latest French fashions.

The problem was that she could not have such things and move beneath Society's notice at the same time.

As much as she longed to be free to love the things she loved, and openly work on causes worth working toward, the world did not allow it. Especially not if one was a marriageable young miss who moved in the exalted circles of the ton.

A spinster, on the other hand, was not expected to simper at wealthy bachelors or giggle her way through every waltz. In another year or two, three at the most, Diana would achieve the status of Lost Cause and all the blessed freedom that came with it.

In the meantime, she had to make do with

wallflower. Yet another of her endless disguises, this one allowed her to seemingly conform to Society's expectations—attend balls, accept invitations—without actually taking part in any meaningful way.

If her behavior made Diana seem odd or antisocial or unwomanly, well, sometimes one must sacrifice one's best pieces in order to win the game. Her only possession Society valued was her reputation. If it were up to Diana, she'd sacrifice that, too. Being "ruined" would make things far simpler, because then she wouldn't have to live a lie in two worlds. She could leave High Society behind and concentrate on everyday people.

Well, if it wouldn't reflect poorly on Thaddeus. He was a dreadful chess player and a delightful cousin. The only reason she bothered playing along at all was because he loved this world. Dancing, dinner parties, pleasure gardens. If escorting her along made him happy, she would not take that away from him.

She'd just watch from the shadows.

Her fingers itched to tug the tiny journal out of her reticule and jot a few notes. Careful observation was the fuel that powered her life. She broke her fast every dawn with a stack of the day's papers, spent the morning on her feet performing firsthand investigations at wine merchants, reviewed and strategized every afternoon in preparation for the evening, in which she would scribble innovations and inefficiencies witnessed from the background of social gatherings.

Lately, however, all of her musings centered on the Duke of Colehaven. Try as she might, she could not get him out of her mind.

Her gaze once again picked him out from the crowd.

The very unremarkableness of his understated attire made the man himself stand out from all the other lords in black coats and white cravats. Colehaven had a *presence* the others did not. A way of parting the room just by entering it, of causing every face to tilt toward his like flowers in search of sunlight. Everyone seemed to bloom as he passed by.

Diana resisted the urge to fluff her gown or twirl a limp tendril of hair into a curl. She had no intention to primp for him, of all people. Her only goal was to remain unnoticed until it was time to go home.

Yet, not for the first time, she felt Colehaven's eyes upon her. Her pulse quickened. Why was he watching? After their disastrous introduction, he would not dare invite her to dance, would he? How would she reply, if he did?

The duke's gaze slid away, as if he had not recognized her at all.

Diana's shoulders slumped against the wall in equal parts relief and chagrin. Of course a devastatingly handsome duke in the middle of a gay ball had not smoked her out from amongst such a splendid crowd.

He was likely on the hunt for a duchess-worthy debutante. Or perhaps on the prowl for another rakish conquest. Diana didn't care. She was watching him because she was bored, not because she had any wish to find herself in his arms.

"I'd rather be in the library," came a voice to her left.

Diana turned her head sharply in surprise. After years of haunting the shadows of Society gatherings, this was one of the few times someone had approached her.

The young lady appeared to be around Diana's age. An inch or two shorter, half a stone lighter, dark hair, brown eyes. A stunning evening gown of midnight blue gauze over an underdress of lavender satin. She was staring at Diana with unabashed interest.

Most likely, they had glimpsed each other on countless other occasions. Unfortunately, for as adept as Diana was at memorizing numbers and performing advanced calculations, she was hopeless at remembering faces.

To combat this lapse, she maintained detailed physical descriptions in her journal of everyone she had ever met. This was not the moment to pull it from her reticule and attempt to determine a match.

"I'd prefer a library, too," she admitted instead, "but that's the first place my guardian would look for me."

The young lady wrinkled her nose in commiseration. "Mine, too."

"You have a guardian?" Diana's mind whirred. Less than one percent of unmarried Society ladies were sponsored wards without immediate family, which meant this woman was either—

"I have a brother," the young lady replied, destroying that hope. "The worst sort of guardian to have. Especially when he's a duke."

Diana narrowed her eyes. "Colehaven?"

"Colehaven," the young lady agreed with a long-suffering sigh.

Diana ground her teeth. No need to open a journal to discover this woman's name. This was Lady Felicity, younger sister—and sole sibling—to the Duke of Colehaven. Who was proving more vexing by the second.

Her fingers curled into fists. "Did your brother send you over here?"

"Yes," Lady Felicity replied without prevarication.

"For what purpose?" Diana demanded. "He cannot desire a formal introduction."

"Not with him," Lady Felicity agreed. "I'm to introduce you to everyone else, particularly the gentlemen."

Diana gaped at her. *"Why?"*

"He didn't say." Lady Felicity lifted a shoulder. "But it appears he intends to matchmake you. Or have me do it, rather."

Over Diana's dead body. The back of her neck flushed with heat. She was not some pitiful project for an arrogant duke to take under his wing, and she definitely wasn't going to allow him to upset her perfectly controlled "wallflower" guise.

Her hackles rose. To the devil with the duke, and he could take his sister with him. Diana had no use for anyone who believed he could march all over someone else's life, and she certainly wasn't going to submit to—

"From here, I can see at least half a dozen eligible bachelors I could introduce you to." Lady Felicity's brown eyes brightened. "Or we could go to the library instead."

A snort of startled laughter escaped before Diana could contain it.

"You don't intend to heed your brother's bidding?"

"My life's work primarily consists of thwarting him at every turn," Lady Felicity replied with an impish grin. "I suppose I could introduce you to all the most *in*eligible bachelors, and count how many minutes he lasts before storming over to demand what the deuce I think I'm doing."

Diana grinned. Such an image was almost tempting. Lady Felicity wasn't what she'd expected after all. If Diana could afford to risk having friends, someone like Lady Felicity wouldn't be a bad start.

Unfortunately, Diana had to nip this nonsense in the bud before her ability to move unnoticed in this crowd was ruined forever.

"The library," she said decisively. It should be vacant enough for a quick conversation to go unremarked. "Can you bring your brother to me?"

"Oh, pooh." Lady Felicity's shoulders sank. "I

was hoping we could hunt for the latest Radcliffe instead."

"You hunt for the Radcliffe," Diana suggested. "I'm going to let your brother know exactly what I think of his meddling."

"On second thought," Lady Felicity said, "I'd rather watch *that*." She dipped into a perfect curtsy. "Lady Felicity Sutton, unexpectedly pleased to make your acquaintance."

"Miss Diana Middleton." With a grin, Diana dipped a curtsy of her own. "Likewise."

If she wondered how Lady Felicity intended to lure her brother to the library, the mystery did not last for long. The moment the two young ladies quit the wainscoting in favor of the ballroom exit, rather than the dance floor, Colehaven immediately abandoned his champagne in pursuit.

Diana and Lady Felicity had only just found the library when Colehaven burst in right behind them.

"Why aren't you in the ballroom?" he demanded.

"Why are you in my business at all?" Diana countered, hands on her hips.

Lady Felicity disappeared among the stacks of books, but Diana rather suspected she was peeking from behind the credenzas.

"What's so hard about meeting other people?"

"I didn't enjoy meeting *you*," Diana snapped, her heart racing. She hadn't noticed how long his eyelashes were before. She couldn't look away from those magnetic hazel eyes.

"I don't enjoy being extorted," he snarled. Or perhaps meant to snarl.

He didn't look angry anymore. In fact, he wasn't looking at her eyes at all. His gaze had dropped a few inches lower, where Diana's teeth nibbled her lower lip.

She licked her lips in response.

He stepped closer.

"I blackmailed you," she stammered, the words coming out far breathier than she intended, "into *not* marrying me."

"Marriage is not what's on my mind." His voice was husky, his mouth suddenly nearer, as if he could not prevent his body from inching closer and closer to hers.

Somehow, her feet were doing the same. When the tip of her toe brushed against his, her shiver had nothing to do with the January weather and everything to do with the irresistible scoundrel before her.

"Queen to H5," she whispered.

"A feint," he murmured, the full intensity of his gaze meeting hers. "My pawn protects me."

Her heart beat faster at the realization that he, too, could visualize a chessboard.

She shook her head. "You lost that pawn in your opening gambit."

"Did I?" he asked softly, lifting his hand toward her face. "Then may the queen defend herself from *this* move."

His thumb touched her cheek.

Diana held her breath.

A pile of books clattered to the floor.

She and Colehaven jumped apart, color flooding both of their faces.

"Sorry!" squeaked a voice on the other side of the closest credenza. "My elbow… I wasn't watching. I mean, I was definitely watching, but not the shelves—"

"Felicity," Colehaven growled, his deep voice rife with warning.

Diana tensed, her runaway pulse still fluttering madly. She'd forgotten all about Lady Felicity. Apparently the duke had, too. There was no disguising the fact that she'd been shamelessly eavesdropping… or that Lady Felicity had flagrantly disregarded every one of her brother's wishes. Her heart skipped in alarm. How would the duke react to such an obvious transgression?

Lady Felicity slunk out from betwixt the stacks with an angelic expression. "Yes, dear brother?"

Colehaven slashed a stern finger in her direction. "*No* lemon tarts. None for the rest of your life. Do you hear me?"

"Worth it," Lady Felicity whispered to Diana as she sashayed out the library with her head held high.

Diana took an extra step backward. Clearly her body could not be trusted not to melt directly into the arms of the enemy.

"I don't have time for… *this*," she mumbled.

"You don't have time for…" He flung his arms wide. "Do you think I've nothing else to do all day but root up suitors for determined wallflowers? I've the Royal Mint to mind—"

"I'm busy, too," she interrupted hotly.

"—and the Consolidated Fund to consider—"

"Which would work better if monies could be appropriated for public works."

"—and smoothing vendor discrepancies regarding the weight and size of their products—"

"If the extremely busy, super important featherwits of the House of Lords would spend as much time on logic as on their mistresses, perhaps England could standardize its units instead of juggling twenty-seven definitions of 'bushel.' Not to mention the peck, the jigger, the pottle, the firkin—"

"That's how measurement *works*." He arched a brow. "Next you'll want to switch from yards to meters."

"Napoleon ridiculed the notion too," she informed him, "but he changed his tune when he realized its efficacy. If multiple countries saw the value after the Congress of Vienna, perhaps it would behoove England to consider—"

"It's never going to happen." His arms folded across his muscular chest. "If you knew how long I fought before we eked through an act meant to hinder the use of false measurements—"

"You were responsible for the 1815 Weights and Measures Act?" she asked in disbelief. "Eighteen years had passed since the last time anyone—"

"I know," he said. "I was there. And no, it

wasn't just me. It was a committee. Do you have any idea how many acts the House of Lords passes each year?"

"One hundred and forty-two last year, one hundred and eighty-two the year before, and one hundred and sixty-two the year before that," Diana said automatically. However, her mind was not on the past, but the future.

Colehaven dragged a hand through his hair and gave her a sideways look. "Are we really standing around arguing about standardizing weights and measures?"

No, Diana realized in wonder. She was done arguing and had no intention of standing about.

The duke was clearly no empty-headed dandy. Whether he realized it or not, the causes he fought for were the same as hers. Not only was he clever enough to comprehend chess, he was a champion of facts and reason.

When it came to reforming irregular systems of measure, he had personally helped drive the first signs of progress in nearly two decades. But there was far more work to be done. A secret grin threatened to take over Diana's face.

The Duke of Colehaven was much more than a handsome nuisance.

He was her ticket to gain entry.

CHAPTER 6

When she'd walked away from the Duke of Colehaven last night, Diana did not yet have a plan.

She was very rarely without a plan. The strange sense of *not knowing* flustered and frustrated her. Had he truly contemplated kissing her? Or was it just another way for him to demonstrate the power he could wield?

Diana shook her head. Kisses did not matter—no matter what her feverish dreams might have contained. What mattered was that she had made the acquaintance of someone in a position to make laws to ensure greater fairness for all citizens.

Granted, he did not yet see things her way. They had started off wrong, obviously. A situation that would have to be rectified if she wished to have any hope of him being open to her input.

Not her *opinion*, mind you. Diana was not one to spout off opinions shilly-shally or let her good sense be swayed by something as mercurial as emotions.

She dealt with empirical observations, direct investigation, painstakingly collected details, absolute fact. And the fact was, the people of England were being swindled on a daily basis. Sometimes due to corrupt agents, and sometimes due to sheer ignorance.

It was all so easily preventable. A uniform system of measurements, coupled with government oversight and consistent enforcement of—

"Doesn't it weigh right?" asked the panicking shopkeeper before her.

"Yes," Diana said quickly. She reassured him with a smile as she gathered her tools back into her basket, alongside her journal and a change of disguise. "Thank you for complying with the law."

His eyes widened. "I would never dream of doing otherwise."

If only all his competitors shared the same high standard.

No, Diana corrected herself as she took her leave from the shopkeeper. If only it were *easier* for ordinary people to adhere to consistent standards.

If she were a member of the House of Lords, the first Act of Parliament she'd argue for would be a complete overhaul of current weights and measures. Today's system was too opaque to enforce, too illogical for many people to follow. Simple, uniform measures would ensure fairness for everyone.

But Diana wasn't a lord. She was a nobody spinster, whose status and gender barred her from championing her own causes or putting forth ideas directly. The most she could provide her fellow citizens was surreptitious inspections and anonymous letters.

So be it. She'd remain a spinster secret agent forever, as long as she could keep making a difference.

She pushed out of the shop and back out onto the street. It was warmer today than yesterday, which meant the light dusting of snow had long since melted into mud. Her nondescript bonnet and coat blended perfectly. One or two more stops, and she could be home long before her cousin awoke.

But when she turned toward St. James, a familiar figure crossed into her view.

Diana could not repress a smile at the sight of Felicity Sutton. For the sister of a duke, Lady Felicity had been a bundle of contradictions. Elegant and impertinent, popular and bookish.

The young lady claimed to prefer the solitude of the library to the swirl of a waltz, yet no expense had been spared in the commission of an ensemble Diana had glimpsed not six weeks earlier in a collection of the newest fashion plates out of Paris.

Diana exchanged her dowdy "measures inspectress" bonnet for the colorful spare inside her basket. Its profusion of silk flowers and wild feathers was just as powerful a disguise. With this outrageous confection tied to her head, no one would remember that the rest of Diana's attire was drab and colorless.

She tightened the ribbon beneath her chin, then turned in Lady Felicity's direction. Within moments, the young lady was nearly upon her.

Lady Felicity's eyes lit up at once. "Miss Middleton! How lovely to see you."

"How lovely to see *you*."

In more ways than one.

Lady Felicity's fashionable walking dress was made of pale green figured muslin with forest green embroidered trim. The sort Diana longed to wear. Lady Felicity's matching spencer fit her frame perfectly and the rakish bonnet added just the right touch of irreverence. She was beautiful.

Diana wished she, too, could be a walking fashion plate. But it was not a fantasy she could indulge.

She would never jeopardize the ability to blend in as a harried under-secretary to some nameless solicitor. Nor could she risk the ton perceiving her as an eligible miss on the marriage mart. A husband would put paid to her extracurricular activities even faster than a spoiled disguise.

"You must be quite an early riser," she ventured. In five years of clandestine missions, this was the first time she'd glimpsed a member of the Quality awake at such an hour, much less out performing errands.

"Not me," Lady Felicity said with a laugh. "My

brother has got it in his head that I spend too much time 'cooped up indoors' and has taken it upon himself to drag me everywhere he goes. Except his tavern, of course. Only ruined women dare enter there."

Diana gave a smile of commiseration. "He sounds much like my cousin. I wouldn't attend Society events at all, were it not for Thaddeus practically tossing me over his shoulder as if I were—"

Amusement quickly turned to apprehension.

"Wait, did you say, your brother? The Duke of Colehaven is here?"

"Haggling over hops just around the corner. It's not the price—Cole could make beer out of gold if he desired. But it seems some magician with a greenhouse managed to grow some sort of delicious, rare varietal that he refuses to part with at any price. Mark my words. No matter how the negotiations are proceeding, as soon as my brother notices me missing, he'll—"

"Felicity Sutton," growled a deep, familiar voice. "I've half a mind to—"

He drew up short when he realized who his sister was speaking to.

Diana wiggled her fingers in greeting, then quickly shoved her hands out of sight. These were her working-woman gloves, not the luxurious ones her cousin had bought her. Best to keep the attention on her face and its ridiculous bonnet—and to cut the conversation as short as possible.

No matter how much she might like to stare at Colehaven all day.

His wide shoulders were barely contained in a coat of grey superfine. His dark hair spilled boyishly from beneath his hat, and his hazel eyes teased and sparkled with their depthless color. Diana could not have looked away if she tried.

"Miss Middleton," he murmured, and made an elegant leg.

She bobbed a belated curtsy. "Your Grace."

He did not seem to notice the forced gaiety of her bonnet or the calculated forgettableness of every other stitch on her body. He did not seem to be interested in her clothing at all. Every ounce of his hot, dark gaze focused on the lower lip she was currently gnawing out of nervousness.

She stopped biting her lip at once.

He did not immediately lift his gaze. When those long-lashed hazel eyes met hers at last, their sultry expression suggested that he, too, had lost precious hours of sleep wondering what might have happened if their lips had been allowed to touch.

Her skin warmed and she immediately glanced away to mask the increased tempo of her pulse. It would not do for him to suspect how he affected her. She must lock that part of herself away with the rest.

Diana had known when she started this path that it would mean choosing between two markedly different lives. She could either be a fashionable young lady with high society beaux and nothing more pressing than to curl her hair in time to make an appearance at Almack's…

Or she could disappear from that world altogether, choosing instead to make a difference in the lives of ordinary citizens, for whom the extra shilling of a deceptive scale might mean the difference between having enough money to eat, or candles to see by.

Diana had made the right choice. She would stand by her convictions.

"You'll be at the Riddings' soirée tomorrow evening, I trust?" Colehaven enquired.

"It depends." Diana bit her lip. Whatever had caused the duke's ill-timed interest in marrying her off, she needed it to stop. "Will you be there?"

Colehaven narrowed his eyes. "Why do I suspect that my attendance would ensure your absence?"

"Because you aren't nearly the simpleton I initially took you for," she assured him.

Felicity snorted behind a silk-gloved hand and feigned great interest in a window display of men's hairbrushes. "Why, are those… boar bristles? Please excuse me whilst I take a closer look."

Diana glared after her. The dratted woman was meant to take her brother with her when she left, not abandon them alone together.

Colehaven took a step closer. "Where's your chaperone?"

Diana gestured vaguely at the shop behind her. This was not the moment to admit she'd brought no such thing in order to perpetuate a false identity.

"Why do you care what I do?" she asked instead.

"I intend to matchmake you," he replied, surprising her with his honesty. "The task becomes exponentially more difficult if you ruin your reputation before a suitor can be found."

"You may call off your search." She folded her arms beneath her bosom. "I don't know why you've decided to meddle in my affairs, but I do not require your services."

He arched a brow. "Says the wallflower whom no one can recall ever seeing on the dance floor."

Diana would feel better if his compatriots could not recall ever seeing her anywhere at all.

"I'm not interested," she said primly.

"Of course you're *interested,*" he said in exasperation. "All young ladies hope to marry well. The longer you wait, the harder it becomes."

Precisely. Diana smiled to herself. In another year or two, she'd be off the marriage mart altogether, and conversations such as this would become moot.

Colehaven shook his head, as if there was nothing so heartbreaking as the thought of her becoming an unshackled spinster with the freedom to do and live as she pleased.

"You've no independent fortune with which to secure your future," he said gently. "There's no shame in accepting help. I wager you'll marry the gentleman I select, and happily."

"I'll take that bet." Diana lifted her chin. "I'm not marrying anyone, least of all some sap *you've* chosen for me."

She cursed her tongue at once. She had not meant to admit her intention to remain unwed. It made her memorable. The duke was right—marrying well was the singular obsession of every other eligible young lady of Diana's acquaintance. Doing so was often the only way to ensure a comfortable future.

"I am in a unique position to provide great service," Colehaven continued. "I know everyone in the ton. If you could give me a hint of what you'd like..."

"*You*," she said at once, "abandoning this ghastly plot."

A husband would be the worst sort of leg-shackle. He would possess all the power, in every sense. Which meant staying as far from the altar as possible. No matter the ache in her chest when she thought of the alternate life she was forsaking.

After all, she didn't have to give up *everything*. Not having a husband to share her bed did not mean she wouldn't share it with anyone. Since she wasn't saving herself for marriage, her "virtue"—or lack thereof—was hers to do with as she pleased.

"Surely you'd agree that a husband offers *some* advantages," Colehaven said.

Perhaps he didn't mean the comment to send shivers of anticipation down her spine. The thought of carnal intimacy combined with his intoxicating proximity was almost too much to bear. She could barely look at him without wondering how his kiss would feel, what his hands might do. There was no need to *marry* a man to sate the call of desire.

With anyone but him, Diana reminded herself quickly. No ton gentlemen need apply. They had too many rules. Too many expectations. And the Duke of Colehaven might be the most dangerous of all.

"I'll consider your thoughts on marriage," she said aloud, "if you'll consider my suggestions for improvements to the current weights and measures system."

He stared at her as if she had just spouted gibberish.

"Uniformity instead of the current hodgepodge," she prompted. "There's an urgent need to simplify and normalize—"

"Yes, yes," he interrupted impatiently. "I recall every word of your argument. It won't convince a single person to switch from yards to meters. Try to focus on the topic at hand."

Diana was more focused than ever.

He remembered every word of her argument? She hadn't believed he was paying attention at all. This development made her dream to bend the ear of Parliament seem… well, perhaps not easily attainable, but at least less far-fetched. She tilted her head and considered him anew.

While most women likely took one look at his sultry, endless hazel gaze and schemed to become his duchess, Diana wished to become something far more impactful: a *colleague*. A sounding-board. A trusted source. When the duke was off crafting laws for the citizens of England, she wanted to be the voice in the back of his mind.

"Cole," his sister called. "Perhaps we could all go to Gunter's for ices?"

"*No*," Diana said quickly. "That is, I very much appreciate the offer, but my cousin and I are otherwise promised."

Colehaven bowed. "Perhaps next time."

Next time.

Hope buoyed her as he led his sister down the street. Diana pressed her hands to her chest. Instead of spending her nights drafting anonymous letters that never received answers, how heady would it be to have a member of Parliament listen to her words and consider her perspective?

She let out a long sigh. A powerful lord welcoming the counsel of an ordinary woman was a situation so unheard of as to be outright fanciful. Yet even the faint possibility of being taken seriously *as herself* was more than she had ever dreamed.

But how would she accomplish such a feat? She had no idea how to gain his ear, much less his trust. A small smile played at the edges of her lips.

This was the perfect opportunity for a bit of reconnaissance.

CHAPTER 7

Within the hour, Diana presented herself at the rear entrance to the Wicked Duke tavern after a few minor adjustments.

Gone was her flamboyant bonnet. Rather than return to her measures inspectress guise, she tucked her hair beneath a mobcap and tied an apron about her waist so that its telltale frill was visible below the hem of her nondescript coat. After draping a threadbare shawl about her shoulders, Diana gathered her basket and prepared to infiltrate the Duke of Colehaven's lair.

Excitement pulsed through her blood. She did not rap upon the half-open servants' door.

She walked right in.

Clinking glasses and murmured laughter filled what appeared to be the primary kitchen. Two lads were washing and drying plates and mugs whilst a trio of women prepared delicious-smelling meals at the stove and in the fire. To the right was a well-stocked scullery. To the left, a brewing chamber. Diana slipped inside.

Except for the copper kettle, most of the equipment was crafted from fine wood. A lad cracked malted barley in one corner, whilst another strained mash into a barrel. Across the room, a brewer stirred the giant copper.

"Jimmy, give me that yeast," he called out.

The two lads glanced up from their tasks with wide, startled eyes. Either neither of them was Jimmy, or they were both too green to know hops from yeast.

"Jimmy," the brewer snapped without looking up. "Yeast, *now*."

Neither lad moved a muscle.

Diana moved closer.

"Where's Jimmy?" she whispered.

"Takin' care of his mum," one of the lads whispered back. "Slipped on a patch of ice, she did. He's afraid he'll lose his post if the master finds out. We're trying to cover for him."

"Good work," Diana murmured. Mums—and friends—ought to be taken care of.

But beer wasn't going to brew itself.

She glanced about the chamber in search of the missing yeast. Taking care to keep her face hidden by the brim of her mobcap, she hastened the yeast to the brewer and handed it up in silence.

He grunted his acceptance without sparing her so much as a glance.

Diana grinned to herself. Apparently servants

were just as unremarkable in taverns as they were in the neighboring shops.

She was not reckless enough to enter the public salons, of course. Even though her cousin was home abed, and the Duke of Colehaven was off chaperoning his sister, it was not worth the risk.

Besides, she hadn't infiltrated the tavern to gawp at its clientele, but rather to research its owner.

If Diana had learned anything in her five years of firsthand investigations, it was that the measure of a man was not in his public persona, but rather in how he conducted his business. She longed to slide her journal from her basket and scribble surreptitious notes as she inspected every element.

Thus far, Diana had every reason to be impressed. With the exception of the absent Jimmy, every member of staff was at his post and performing his job admirably. The shelves were well-stocked and neatly organized, each post designed for a specific position or task.

She glanced over as two maids entered, apparently having just come from market. With brisk efficiency, they set several heavy baskets on a narrow kitchen table and began to unload their bounty.

One of them furrowed a quizzical brow toward Diana. "Who're you?"

"Mrs. Flanders," she improvised with authority, as if that answered the question. She arched her brows. "Were you able to purchase all the necessary supplies?"

The maid nodded, her mind clearly on other tasks. "The usual, plus provisions for tonight."

"What's tonight?" Diana asked. Now that the maids assumed she'd been charged with inspecting the kitchen, she could not allow such a singular opportunity to go to waste.

The maid looked at her as if she'd lost her mind. "Scotch collops, veal, roast wigeons, stewed celery, sweetbreads, peas, and tartlets. It's Thursday."

"Of course," Diana murmured.

The elder maid pushed a square of parchment in her direction. "Check it yourself."

Diana accepted the paper.

She immediately pulled her weights and scales from her basket and placed them on the table. One by one, she weighed each of the purchases and compared the results with the expected weight indicated on the paper.

Most of the items balanced perfectly.

Three did not.

"Where did you get this cream?" she demanded. "And this barley? And these peas?"

The younger maid turned over the paper to reveal a crude map on the other side.

"Not everyone's there all the time, but there's the best peas—" She pointed to a small X. "—and the best barley—" She pointed to another X. "—and the cheapest cream."

No wonder the cream was inexpensive. The

vendor had given the maid short measure, either by placing a surreptitious finger on the scale, or having an incorrectly calibrated scale in the first place.

The peas likewise fell under the desired weight, but the barley was slightly over. Either the vendor had been generous to two pretty maids, or the person he swindled every day was himself.

Diana copied the map to her journal and added appropriate notations. She would ensure her future list included each of these vendors. Regardless of whether the Duke of Colehaven proved to be the sort of man a woman could converse with about weight distribution and mathematical accuracy, Diana could not allow him or his kitchen staff to be cheated out of a single pea.

She returned the slip of paper to the maids just as the sound of loud laughter filled the other half of the tavern.

"Midday, then," the elder maid muttered without glancing at a time piece.

The younger one nodded in commiseration. "Queue starts at half past eleven."

"Their Graces will be here within the hour." The elder maid pointed at the celery. "Start chopping."

Diana's spine snapped up straight in alarm.

Their Graces could only mean the tavern's owners, the original wicked dukes: Colehaven and Eastleigh. Diana had never met the Duke of Eastleigh, but she could not risk still being present when the Duke of Colehaven arrived.

Yet the voices that spilled through the open doorway leading from the kitchen to the primary salon were impossible to resist. She would not make a return visit to the tavern. This was her last chance to observe firsthand the character of its clientele.

Careful to stay out of sight, she moved closer to the open door and listened.

"I disagree," said a male voice. "Defining the pound sterling relative to gold was the wisest act Parliament made last year."

Diana blinked. This was definitely not the drunken banter she had feared.

"Don't let Colehaven hear you go on about it," said another. "You'll fill his head with flowers."

"That was one of his?" The first man asked.

"On the committee," a third voice confirmed. "Don't you remember when he barely stayed for more than a pint before going off to shut himself in his office to rewrite drafts?"

"No," the first man said with a laugh. "I drank *my* pints. Can't recall a thing."

Glasses clinked together.

With a little smile, Diana shook her head and turned to go.

"Think he'll have married off that Middleton chit by now?" asked another voice.

Diana froze in place.

"He's on a winning streak, isn't he?" Said one of the men. "Besides, I hear she's comely enough, if you catch sight of her."

"Mayhap," another said slowly. "Then again,

didn't Thaddeus claim she was nigh unmarriageable?"

"Not 'nigh' unmarriageable," corrected his friend. "*Unmarriageable.*"

Diana swayed, her head dizzy. *Thad* said that? Her stomach sank. He wasn't just her guardian. He was her cousin and only friend. Everyone thought of them as practically siblings. Diana loved him like a brother.

And he could not wait to be rid of her.

"That's as may be," said another. "But Colehaven would not have agreed to the scheme unless he was confident he'd come through a winner. I imagine he has a whole host of potential suitors in mind."

Her stomach sank. The news was worse by the second.

"Wager you're right," said the first man. "Colehaven's probably drafting up marriage contracts as we speak."

She curled her shaking fingers into fists. To the devil with the duke's potential suitors—and her cousin's lack of faith in her worth. She was no man's pawn.

Diana definitely wasn't going to be married off against her will because some self-righteous duke believed he knew what she wanted better than she did. Or maybe he didn't care what she wanted at all. She was just a wager. Another notch on his fancy winning streak.

Without a word, she stalked out through the

kitchen and into the sunlight. A grim smile curved her lips.

The Duke of Colehaven believed himself capable of playing puppet-master over Diana's life? He had vastly underestimated his opponent.

She'd be the one to play *him*.

CHAPTER 8

Cole strode through the main entrance of the Wicked Duke with his brow furrowed in thought.

"Colehaven!" came the rallying cry. A dozen mugs toasted him in unison.

He took his usual seat amongst the usual crew, but little about his life seemed usual anymore. He didn't even want the frothy ale the barkeep slid in his direction. Instead of drinking, Cole glared at the monogrammed mug in silence.

"Why the scowl?" Jack Barrett asked. "Your sister take apart your curricle again?"

"Worse," Giles Langford teased. "He's been sacked from the Proper Planting of Plums committee."

Cole *wished* he was on a plum committee. Perhaps then his brain would have something productive to ruminate upon, rather than replay every maddening moment of his interactions with Diana Middleton.

When Thad had claimed his ward was unmarriageable, Cole had assumed her lack of suitors was due to a plain countenance, or slow-wittedness, or perhaps some sort of clumsiness that kept her from being a desirable dance partner. Green bucks were often superficial in their requirements for a wife.

But the lady was beautiful, clever, surefooted, sure-everythinged. If she lacked suitors, Cole now suspected she had frightened them off on purpose.

"Well?" Eastleigh drawled.

"Diana Middleton," Cole muttered, and lifted his ale to his lips before he could be prevailed upon to clarify.

"He's losing?" Someone blurted out in disbelief.

"Check the book," someone else shouted in delight. "I put ten quid on an end to the winning streak!"

"I'm not *losing*." Cole set down his ale. "I have until the end of the season, which you might recall only began this week."

"Definitely losing," Eastleigh stage-whispered, to the crowd's delight.

Cole glared at his best friend.

Eastleigh clinked his mug against Cole's. "May all the women in your life never give you a moment's peace."

"May the one who got away find her way back," Cole shot back.

Eastleigh choked on his ale.

"Another round," Langford called out.

"And a bib for Eastleigh!" someone else shouted.

Everyone was laughing again, including Cole. He couldn't help it. No matter what was going on outside, the Wicked Duke always put him in a fine mood.

The tavern was more than just a familiar haven where everyone knew his name, and was pleased to see him every time he walked through the door. He'd enjoyed their company for years. He *knew* them; and they him. A simple thing, but one Cole took great comfort in.

When he'd first arrived in Oxford, he'd been "befriended" by a group of Janus-faced lads who mocked Cole behind his back at every turn. Everything marked him as an outsider. His accent, his discomfort in his clothes, his occasional failure to respond when addressed by his new title, to realize that "Your Grace" referred to *him*. To that lot, he'd been nothing more than an object of ridicule.

Meeting Eastleigh and his friends had changed everything.

Suddenly, Cole found himself surrounded by lads who were exactly who they presented themselves to be. Rogues, every last one of them. Cole and Eastleigh were the worst of the lot. Genuine, honest, and unapologetically mischievous. They'd earned the moniker "wicked dukes" and lived up to their reputations. Not just as impish scoundrels, but also as formidable opponents in the classroom and out.

He'd sworn never to waste time with two-faced hypocrites ever again.

Cole no longer remembered who had dared them to open a tavern and call it the Wicked Duke. He was just glad they had. The unpretentious public house had succeeded far beyond anyone's expectations.

"To the Wicked Duke," he said and lifted his mug.

"To the Wicked Duke!" his friends chorused back.

Cole grinned and took a swig of ale.

"What are you going to do with Miss Middleton?" Eastleigh murmured.

An image of plump, rosy lips and teasing blue eyes filled him with sudden want.

"Nothing," he managed, unable to wipe the tantalizing image from his mind. "Marry her off."

"I assume you've prepared a list of likely candidates."

Cole lifted his beer rather than reply.

He did not have a list of likely candidates prepared. In fact, the thought of her opening her arms to some other man raised the hackles on the back of his neck.

"Not all men are created equal," he muttered. "I have to ensure he's worthy."

Eastleigh snorted. "You're supposed to find her a good match, not hold out for a fairytale prince to come whisk her away to his castle."

Cole had the sneaking suspicion he wouldn't care much for the fairy prince, either. Not that it mattered. He'd taken the bet, and was playing to win.

He would find Diana Middleton a match.

CHAPTER 9

At the Riddings' soirée the following night, Diana assumed her usual spot along the wall farthest from the dancing. The Jacobean Oak of the Riddings' wainscoting prevented her from truly blending with the background, but she'd taken care to select a gown whose pale blue color matched the wall hangings perfectly.

Diana prepared for a long evening of protracted invisibility. She was never bored; analyzing the notes in her journal kept her mind happily occupied. Soirées were also splendid opportunities to observe ton exchanges undetected.

At least, they used to be.

To Diana's surprise, the wainscoting had been digging into her spine for scarcely a quarter hour before a trio of fashionable young ladies headed straight to her refuge, with Felicity Sutton leading the way.

"Do *not* try the lemonade," Lady Felicity whispered as she handed Diana a glass of sherry. "Unless you enjoy the shock of undiluted lemon juice without the slightest hint of sugar, that is."

Diana blinked. "I…"

Lady Felicity gestured to the young lady on her right. "This is Lady Viola Fairfax. Our brothers own the Wicked Duke, but please don't hold it against us." Lady Felicity gestured to her left. "This is Miss Priscilla Weatherby. Her parrot can swear in three languages." She grinned at her friends. "Pris, Vi, this is Miss Diana Middleton. I witnessed her tongue-lash Colehaven and live to tell the tale. She's one of us."

Diana's throat tightened. She'd never had an *us* to belong to before. The sensation almost made her dizzy.

Although the last thing she needed was an exponential increase in members of high society who could recognize her, Diana could not help a flutter of wistfulness in her belly at the idea of having friends. Of being part of an *us*.

"How do you do," she stammered belatedly.

Now that they'd met her, the best thing to do was not to call further attention. She would present herself as ordinary, boring, unremarkable. Within a few days' time, something more interesting would attract their attention, and Diana would return to her usual wallflowerdom.

"Have you any plans tomorrow afternoon?" Lady Felicity asked. "We're going to Bond Street for new gloves, then to the park for ice-skating."

"Unless it rains," Lady Viola added.

Lady Felicity nodded. "If it rains, I'll spend the

entire afternoon before a fire with a pot of chocolate and my copy of *Glenarvon*. I've almost deduced the true identities of each of the characters."

Lady Viola pulled a face. "Bad form to gossip about one's peers."

"But delicious reading," Lady Felicity said with an unrepentant grin. "I once believed myself a hoyden, but I now realize I'll have to work much harder if I'm to be satirized in a gothic novel someday."

Miss Weatherby choked on a laugh. "If Colehaven heard you say such a thing—"

"—I would unleash Miss Middleton upon him." Lady Felicity sent Diana a conspiratorial wink. "He doesn't scare her one whit."

A perfect storm of warring emotions battled in Diana's chest. She longed to be part of such a lively, laughing group. To go ice-skating, to shop together, to exchange books and giggle over private jests.

But that was a different life than the one she had chosen. A different woman. She needed to remain in the background, to be the sort of person one's eyes might notice but never quite *see*.

In such a position, only a fool would spend a moment more than necessary in the company of a young lady who prided herself on her ability to unmask true identities. If Diana's double life became common knowledge, her reputation would be ruined—and perhaps Thad's as well, by association.

The best thing for Diana and these smiling young ladies was to go their separate paths.

Yet how was Diana meant to shoo them off without arousing even greater intrigue?

Miss Weatherby glanced over her shoulder. "Where *is* Colehaven?"

Diana's eyes immediately flicked to the duke's precise location. She had been aware of him from the moment she and her cousin had entered the ballroom.

It was more than merely being the most handsome man present. It was as if every inch of her body was attuned to his every move. A flash of a smile warmed her insides. A rumble of a laugh set her heart aflutter.

Nerves, Diana told herself. Nothing more. A duke was dangerous on general principle, but a lord who appeared to be close personal friends with every person he passed was even more so. His interest in her was predicated solely on a dare. Likely he was canvassing his peers to determine which poor cretin was the one he could foist her off on.

Oh, why did he have to make that wager? A member of the House of Lords acknowledging the passionate opinions of an unwed, untitled, unimportant young lady was a long shot in the best of circumstances. With the duke's attention consumed with winning a bet, he would be even less open to long discussions of politics or the painstaking research she'd charted by hand in her journals.

"I'll wave him over," Lady Felicity said, and immediately lifted her fan to catch her brother's eye.

Colehaven's gaze snapped not to his sister, but to Diana.

"Excuse me," Diana blurted. "I have to go."

She handed back the sherry and fled the ballroom before the young ladies could ask any questions. Diana hated to be rude, but nor could she risk the duke and his sister and her friends joining forces in a mission to force her to the dance floor in hopes of meeting her future betrothed.

That was someone else's dream. Not Diana's.

Blindly, she passed the corridor leading to the terrace, the ladies' retiring room, several closed doors, and then caught sight of a dimly lit library. The door was barely ajar, and the only light seemed to emanate from a dwindling fire behind a far grate.

Perfect.

She ducked inside, slipped past the shelves of books to the remains of a fire, and settled on a worn Chesterfield to jot her latest observations in her journal.

Before her fingers could wrest the small volume from her reticule, movement caught the corner of her eye as a certain handsome gentleman penetrated her sanctuary. The duke had found her in the darkness.

"Are you so afraid that someone might dare request your dance card?"

Diana shivered as the low rumble of his voice enveloped her like a caress. Just knowing he shared the firelight with her made her skin flush with heat.

She leapt to her feet, determined to ignore such flights of fancy.

"I don't carry a dance card," she shot back. Or meant to shoot. Now that she saw how little space separated them, she wasn't certain sound had escaped her throat at all.

His body was so close, she could nearly feel his heat against her skin. His dark curls seemed invitingly touchable, his mouth a decadent promise. A risk she dare not take.

Diana swallowed hard. Five years ago, when she'd first decided to serve her country rather than a husband, a tiny part of her had thrilled at the idea of a future filled with undreamed of freedoms.

At the spinster-adjacent advanced age of five-and-twenty, her marriage prospects were already grim. By dispensing with the notion of saving herself for a husband, the exciting possibility of *not* saving anything at all had occurred to her. A woman could sow wild oats as well as any man, could she not? Independence did not imply a life devoid of pleasure.

The fantasy, of course, had been short-lived. Inviting rakes and rogues into her boudoir would have put her too much in the eye of the ton. Eschewing high society dandies for working men wouldn't do either. Not when she needed to present the picture of a professional, unmemorable measures inspectress.

Diana's liaisons with strapping, virile men would remain as fictional as the stories told in the leather-bound novels upon the library shelves.

All of which put her at a distinct disadvantage. She knew everything there was to know about weights and measures and volumes and scales. The one thing she didn't know was what to do with Colehaven.

Or the way the mere sight of him set her pulse aflutter.

She smoothed her gown, grateful for the limited firelight. "If you've come hoping to haul me back to the ballroom to simper at suitors, I'm afraid you've wasted your time."

"I suspected as much," he admitted. "I came anyway."

"Why?" she asked, expecting him to perhaps gently explain why her hopes and thoughts and dreams were completely wrong and how she should let him dictate when and who she should marry.

"Sometimes I'd rather be anywhere but a dance floor, too," he replied.

Diana blinked in surprise. "But you're a duke!"

"Dukes are known for dancing?" he asked with obvious amusement. "Most of them are twice my age and wouldn't be able to find the orchestra with a quizzing glass."

"I meant," she stammered, "aren't heirs and spares groomed for ton life? I would imagine parties of any size to be second nature."

"I'm certain it would have been," he agreed. "If

I had been raised as part of it. My sister and I were the dreaded 'poor relations.' Few people even knew I was distantly in line for the title."

"What happened?" she asked softly.

He paused. "May I?"

She settled on the edge of her chair.

After seating himself, he placed his glass of sherry on the side table rather than bring it to his lips. His expression was pensive.

"Most lords bear many heirs in order to avoid their exalted title falling into the hands of some wretched second or third cousin," he began.

She nodded, frowning.

"I'm the wretched cousin." His honesty was stark. "One day, an unfamiliar barrister informed me that there had been a series of tragedies over the past decade—"

"You hadn't seen your family in a decade?" she blurted out.

"I saw my sister every day. She's my family. No one else ever came to call, perhaps out of fear we would return the gesture." His tone hardened. "No one was more shocked than me. I had no idea how to be a lord, and suddenly I was a duke."

She leaned closer. "What did you do?"

"Learned quickly," he replied. The edges of his mouth curved, but shadows hid whether his smile reached his eyes. "I was sent off for a proper education."

"And was it?"

This time, he did laugh. "More than anticipated, I'd wager. I was completely unprepared, but threw myself into my studies. I had to learn everything I'd missed in order to understand what was being taught. I'm not sure I slept those first few months, so determined was I to at least be recognized as an academic equal."

"The other lordlings believed you unworthy of your title?"

He inclined his head. "Unworthy of Oxford. Inferior to them. So I took it upon myself to excel in every way possible. At first, I thought that meant proving myself better than all the lads who laughed behind my back. They might have been born into their roles, but I was determined to study and practice and memorize until I could out-duke the brightest star among them."

"Did it work?"

"In mysterious ways." His mouth twisted. "I gained their respect at the expense of my own. I finally realized I was allowing the wrong people to determine the worth of a man."

She nodded. "The wrong scale."

He lifted a shoulder. "I wanted to be respected for who I *was,* not by the labels I received by others. I was tired of those constraints. So I broke free."

She arched a brow. "How does one do that?"

"In my case?" He winced. "An exceedingly foolish dare that led me to my first true friend at Oxford."

Diana placed her hands to her temples and feigned concentration. "The spirit guides tell me… the Duke of Eastleigh?"

He widened his eyes. "You should have a fortune-telling tent at Vauxhall. Tell me, will I meet a beautiful stranger?"

"Yes," she said at once. "His name is Eastleigh."

He shook his head as if fondly recalling past exploits. "In no time, we were known as the 'wicked dukes.' We lived up to the name, I'm afraid. Whenever we weren't at our studies—or being wicked—we could be found at a local tavern we'd made our second home."

"Drinking and carousing from dusk till dawn?"

"Worse." He dropped his voice to a whisper. "Drinking and carousing with non-titled persons, *even if they did not attend university.*"

Diana reeled back in mock horror. "Egad!"

He nodded solemnly. "We made friends with half the town before the first year was through. Those drunken debates and spirited conversations introduced me to some of the best men I've ever met."

"I suppose that's why so many men love to pass their days at their clubs."

"No," Colehaven said slowly. "I don't think it is. Most gentlemen's clubs are meant for likeminded individuals of similar tastes and backgrounds. Brooks's is for Whigs, White's for Tories. If any member believes an applicant fails to fit the mold, a single black ball will bar the unwanted element from entry."

"What are the rules for membership in the Wicked Duke?"

"The only rule is that there aren't any rules."

His grin was infectious. "The world may not be equitable for all men, but at least our tavern can be. Regardless of color, creed, or the size of one's coin purse."

Diana's heart warmed. She admired that he strove to create an open forum where multiple classes were not only welcome, but free to share their views and make friends with people wholly different from themselves. It spoke to his character... and filled her with hope.

If she could prove to him an overhaul of England's weights and measurements system wasn't just the logical decision but the *right* thing to do, Colehaven would be the sort of man to stop at nothing to see it through.

She'd done it once, she reminded herself. Her anonymous letters to the House of Lords eventually spurred the Act of 1815. No one suspected the connection, of course. Men might be equal in Colehaven's tavern, but women weren't equal anywhere.

There was no chance of Diana's perspective being respected on its own merit, no matter how much she might wish her thoughts to be seen as valid. If the restructuring was Colehaven's idea, it would have a chance. He might not be ready to join her in a political debate, but surely this evening proved they did not have to be enemies.

He made a face at his wineglass. "Believe it or not, I didn't come here to blather on about the good old days at Oxford."

"The beginning sounded miserable," she assured him with a smile. "If I was uninterested, I would not have asked questions."

If anything, her fingers had itched to slide her journal from its hiding spot and scratch down every word he said in order to analyze it later.

"Then I hope turnabout is fair play," he said with a wry smile. "I came here because I wanted to know more about you."

A sudden rush of fear squeezed the breath from her lungs. The last thing she needed was a powerful duke attempting to uncover personal secrets.

"There's nothing to tell," she said quickly. "I'm sure if there was anything of interest about me, Thaddeus would already have told you."

"I haven't asked," Colehaven admitted. "I wouldn't want him to misconstrue my interest."

Well. *That* bucket of cold water ought to calm her ardor. They might or might not discuss mathematics someday, but the duke's interest in her was merely as an object of curiosity. Lest Diana forget, Colehaven's sole motivation was marrying her off to someone else in order to win a wager.

She set down her glass and rose to her feet. "I should get back before he notices my absence."

Colehaven rose to his feet at once. "Would you like me to escort you?"

"No," she said crisply. "I wouldn't want anyone to misconstrue your interest."

He winced. "That was thoughtless of me. What I meant—"

"Don't misconstrue my interest, either." Her

pulse fluttered in her throat at his nearness. "I don't want to *marry* you."

He took a step closer. "What *do* you want from me?"

She allowed her hungry gaze to rake his form. "I…"

The edge of his boot brushed her slipper and suddenly he was far too close for conscious thought at all.

"Stop me," he said as he lowered his mouth toward hers. "Before I take what *I* want."

In reply, she lifted her lips to meet his.

Electricity raced through her, sending tingles throughout her body. Suddenly her fingers were laced about his neck as his arms cradled her flush to his body.

Until this moment, Diana had believed herself jaded. She'd been kissed before. Nothing could surprise her.

But Colehaven set her flesh ablaze. His touch was nothing like the fumbling stolen kisses of her youth. He was confident, strong, secure. His arms were tight about her, both protective and possessive. Any restraint she'd once believed within her control vanished with the taste of his kiss.

He was heat and passion, freedom and danger. Everything she wanted and could never have, wrapped up in an irresistible package her fingers itched to unwrap. He gave as much as he took, filling her with his taste and scent and touch, leaving her breathless for more.

This was not a kiss. This was a fight for dominance. Temptation to surrender. A reckless promise of untold pleasures, and a warning that to sample them could leave her heart in tatters. Yet she was powerless to resist the pull of desire. Her body swayed at the thought of submitting to his mouth, to his hands, to his—

"Diana?" called a confused voice. "Are you in here?"

She and Colehaven flew out of each other's arms, eyes wide with panic. Diana's lips hummed with the taste of his kiss. Her trembling legs barely kept her upright. The pounding of her heart still rushed in her ears. But none of that mattered. Thaddeus was here, and if he caught them together…

"Hide," she hissed to the duke, placing her palms upon his chest to shove him behind the closest stack of books.

Even that simple touch nearly undid her.

With a final piercing gaze full of words neither of them could say, Colehaven melted into the shadows.

"There you are," scolded Thaddeus as he strode into view. "Could you not hear me calling?"

She slipped her journal from her reticule and flashed its cover toward her cousin. "You know how I am when I'm writing."

"You could fill a library of your own with as many journals as you keep," Thaddeus agreed with a fond smile. He held out his elbow. "Come along, then."

"Am I missed on the dance floor?" she teased.

It was an old joke between them, but even as she said the words, Diana realized the humor was no longer there.

She was not Thad's little wallflower cousin. She was his albatross. His cross to bear. A burden so disappointing, he had felt forced to enlist the aid of his most powerful acquaintance in a desperate attempt to rid himself of her once and for all.

"I shan't make you dance," he said with a little sigh. "I've summoned the carriage. We can go home."

Home. Diana had hoped it would be so for the rest of her life. Knowing her cousin did not feel the same twisted shards of ice in her heart.

When the carriage arrived, he handed her in without a cross word and bounded inside to join her.

Diana loved her cousin. She could no longer keep her silence.

"I'm sorry I am not what society expects me to be," she mumbled. "What you need me to be."

She did not regret the path she'd chosen for herself, or all the positive change she had and would create for her fellow citizens. But she hated that doing so fractured her relationship with the sole family member she had left.

Brow lined with concern, Thaddeus took her hands. "I don't want you to please *me*. I want you to find someone who pleases *you*. It's what you deserve. What everyone deserves. As soon as you're happily married, I will do the same."

Diana's throat was too tight for a response to form. Her cousin's well-wishes squeezed her heart.

This was so much worse than being a disappointment. She was holding back *his* life. As her guardian, he felt it his duty to see her safely settled. By refusing to do so, she was preventing him from finding the love he craved.

Even if she could somehow convince him not to wait for her, to keep searching until he found his perfect match, she could not be the anchor weighing down their happy union. Diana had reached the age of majority. She could not presume to remain her cousin's ward forever.

Sooner rather than later, she would need to be gone.

CHAPTER 10

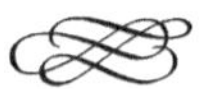

Cole awoke with the taste of Miss Middleton's kiss still haunting his lips. He dressed, broke his fast, attempted to concentrate on the morning paper. But it was no use. His brain could focus on nothing but the delicious memory of last night's stolen moment.

He should not have kissed her. If he'd possessed the least suspicion that she would welcome, rather than spurn, such reckless behavior, perhaps he would not have… oh, who was he bamming? Cole rubbed a hand over his face and sighed.

If he'd believed she intended to kiss him back, he would only have kissed her all the sooner.

Even in the harsh light of day, he could not bring himself to be sorry he had done so. If her cousin had not spoiled the moment, Cole would happily still be in the library right now, his arms about Miss Middleton's warm curves and his mouth enjoying hers. The last thing on his mind had been *stopping*.

It wouldn't do, of course. The terms of the wager required him to match Miss Middleton with some other gentleman. A love match, he'd boldly assured her guardian. Right after agreeing not to publicly influence the outcome by feigning interest in order to manipulate other gentlemen's perceptions.

The kiss had not been public.

Nor had it been feigned.

Cole could not allow such a lapse in judgment to repeat. What the devil had he been thinking?

That she was beautiful and maddening and clever. That moments with her were completely unpredictable. That he could not live another moment without knowing the taste of her lips.

"Imbecile," he muttered.

Something had to be done. He summoned his carriage and directed the coachman toward the Wicked Duke. The tavern would not open for a few more hours, but the familiar drive might help to clear his head.

The sooner he found a worthy match for Miss Middleton, the sooner he could have done with the wager and put all of his attention toward Parliament.

Being chosen to replace Lord Fortescue as committee leader required far more than luck. He needed to be a viable candidate. Strategic and clever, conservative and steady. The sort of man who would not embroil himself in embarrassing scandal. Such as stealing kisses from a woman he had no intention to wed.

There. That put paid to the matter. Cole would not be on the hunt for a bride until the following year, at the earliest, which meant absolutely no roguery with proper young ladies until he was prepared to marry one.

"Wicked Duke," called his driver as he pulled the horses to a stop. "Where to now?"

Cole exchanged a crooked grin with the coachman. This was far from the first drive they'd taken without any particular destination in mind.

"Home, please."

Within seconds, the horses were once again on the move.

Often when Cole needed to think, watching London trundle by did him a world more good than staring at the walls of his study. Particularly if he was ruminating a matter for Parliament. Putting eyes on the very people he was trying to serve kept his focus sharp.

There was never any reason to exit the carriage, because the decisions he needed to reach were located within his mind. More often than not, he was back home within the hour, refreshed and—

"Stop!" he barked, his nose nearly crushing against the carriage window when the coachman immediately obeyed his command.

Perhaps the morning sun slanting across the glass distorted his judgment, but Cole could swear that the plain-clothed woman striding unaccompanied down an alleyway between two buildings was none other than Miss Middleton.

"*Stop,*" he said again, but did not know whether he was speaking to the baffling Miss Middleton or his own galloping heart.

"Wait here," he instructed the driver and leaped from the coach.

Carriages, horses, and carts crossed the busy road, blocking Cole's path—and his view. When at last he could cross the street in pursuit of Miss Middleton, she was no longer visible to the eye.

Swearing beneath his breath, Cole hurried in the direction he'd last glimpsed her.

Perhaps nothing was amiss. Perhaps there was a perfectly reasonable explanation for a proper young lady to be dressed in drab muslin, wandering alone in empty alleyways hours before her genteel counterparts would even open their eyes.

Or perhaps something was very wrong, and she needed his help.

Cole sprinted down the alley and drew up short when it terminated between two storefronts. To the right, a milliner. To the left, a hostel.

He ducked into the milliner's shop. While he could not fathom what urge might spur a young lady to purchase a new bonnet at half eight in the morning, it was the only explanation.

Miss Middleton was nowhere inside.

He spun back out to the alley and narrowed his eyes at the tavern next door. Although he had never frequented this particular establishment, it was known to sell ale by the cup or the gallon, and had an inexpensive menu to accompany one's libation.

But what on earth could any of that have to do with Miss Middleton?

Perhaps he'd been mistaken. The woman he'd seen hadn't been her at all, but rather some matron or housekeeper or headmistress whose own kitchen was inoperable for some reason, forcing her to visit an establishment such as this in order to break her fast.

He pushed open the door and stepped inside, anyway. Just in case.

As with the milliner's, Miss Middleton was nowhere to be seen. In fact, the dining salon was empty of customers and employees alike. Perhaps Cole had hallucinated the entire charade.

But then he heard an unmistakable female voice emanating from a rear room. The murmur was immediately followed by a man's baritone.

Cole was across the dining salon and barging into the private chamber before his brain even had a chance to think.

The male voice appeared to belong to the tavern's owner. The female voice, none other than Miss Middleton. As for what they were doing…

Their heads were bent over a hogshead of beer. The manager's thick arms were folded over his barrel chest. In one of Miss Middleton's slender hands was a mug of ale.

Both sets of eyes widened in surprise at Cole's interruption.

"What are you doing here?" Miss Middleton stammered.

"What the devil are *you* about?" he demanded in reply.

"Mrs. Peabody is tuning our scales," said the owner. "Did you come to join her for breakfast?"

Cole gaped at them both. "Mrs. Peabody?"

"I'm afraid I cannot dine today, Mr. Smith," Miss Middleton said smoothly. "But you're absolutely right. This batch of ale has a far more balanced flavor than the last."

Cole's tongue was thick with confusion. "Balanced… flavor?"

"Well, now, that's thanks to you, Mrs. Peabody," the owner replied, his pale cheeks flushing in pleasure. "You were right about the proportion of hops to barley, and which source currently has the best crop."

Each word seemed to tip the world further off-kilter.

"You improved his ale recipe?"

"And the ingredients," the owner said with pride. "We now brew with the finest barley available to London."

Cole blinked. "Not the Nicholson farm?"

Mr. Smith beamed back at him. "The very one."

Cole spun toward Miss Middleton in befuddlement. "But how would you know—"

She looped her arm through his and pivoted toward the door. "That'll do, I believe. Mr. Smith, Thank you for your hospitality."

"Come back anytime," he called after them.

The moment they were out of the tavern and into the relative sunlight of the alley, Cole turned Miss Middleton to face him. "Mrs. Peabody, is it?"

"It's actually Diana," she murmured. "To my friends."

"I am not your friend," he told her firmly. "I am your self-appointed chaperone until further notice because whoever is *supposed* to be your duenna is not up to the task."

She lifted her chin. "I do not require your help. In fact, your presence is a hindrance."

"A hindrance to what?"

She sighed. "Our system of weights and measures is broken. Hundreds of dishonest vendors cheat their clients every day, stealing from unwitting customers without recompense because absolutely nothing is done to—"

"Nothing is done?" Cole's neck began to heat. "I personally pushed for reform that enacted better laws just two years ago. It's not as though London has a list of known villains that we're willfully ignoring—"

"It is *exactly* as though London has a list, because I wrote it myself!" Miss Middleton snapped. "I write a new report every month, including indexes for and updates to the miscreants mentioned in past missives. I am in a singular position of authority on the matter, and Act or no Act, you haven't done enough!"

"How are you an authority?" he asked. "Who is the real Mrs. Peabody?"

"Mrs. Peabody is the harried under-secretary of a litigious barrister," Miss Middleton bit out, "and she doesn't exist. The problems do, however, and so do the solutions."

He sighed. "Meters again?"

"I'd settle for *logic*. What are we meant to do with three different pipes of wine, two hogsheads, wine gallons that match the weight of a corn gallon filled with wheat… And let's not even touch the twenty-seven styles of bushel. Your lot needs to come up with a system that works, and then *enforce* it."

"You're right," he said. "That's *my* lot. Not the business of a proper young lady with a reputation to keep."

"I've an unblemished reputation," she assured him. "Miscreants shake in their boots and the rest toast my arrival. I know every vendor in London. Where to buy, where not to buy, who to trust, and who would swindle his own mother. They love me or they fear me."

"That is *not* a good reputation," he informed her. "That is the sort of thing that will prevent you from finding—"

She slammed her fists to her hips. "If you say 'a husband,' I shall be forced to violence, so help me God."

He couldn't believe she was fighting him on this. A good marriage wasn't just the best way for a young lady to ensure her future. It was often the *only* way. And he was trying to help!

He stepped closer. "A good match—"

"Bah. When will it occur to you that not all women have no ambitions beyond serving a husband? Before you say 'what else would you do?' please recall that one out of every four women never marries. Are some spinsters overset with sadness at such a gothic fate? Surely. Do other independent women awaken every morning thanking the heavens for another day's freedom?"

"You are not an independent woman," he reminded her. "You are the ward of—"

"I'm five-and-twenty," she said firmly. "Thad is a kind and generous cousin, but he no longer holds legal guardianship. If I had enough wealth, I could rent my own apartment and—"

"*If*," he repeated. "In the absence of independent means, Thaddeus Middleton is your practical guardian, regardless of legal obligation. A woman in your position can either find a man to marry, or pursue genteel employment as a governess or companion. What she can*not* do is—"

"—become an agent of change when she encounters inequity or criminal activity?" she interrupted, eyes flashing. "Have a positive impact on the world around her, at a level outside the home? Be seen and heard and *matter*?"

"Do you think mothers don't matter?" he countered. "That wives don't matter?"

"Having enough bread to eat matters, yet you haven't rushed off to become a baker or a grain harvester." She lifted her chin. "You're most useful in the House of Lords, and I'm most useful as a covert agent out on the streets avenging misapplied mathematics."

"As a covert... that is not a thing that exists!" he spluttered.

"I'm the first one," she said with a shrug. "When I see unfairness, I do my best to fix it. Sometimes the problem lies with undereducated buyers and sometimes an unethical shopkeeper is at fault. One cannot know until firsthand inquiries are made. But if I find a discrepancy... I settle the score."

"It's not the same." He crossed his arms. "Parliament governs with honesty and transparency. Members of the public can view important proceedings from the galleries—"

"Male members of the public," she murmured.

"On the authority of no one at all, you wrap yourself in lies and disguises—"

"It's the only way I can accomplish anything at all." She took a deep breath. "You are privileged to be *able* to be yourself, to force people to notice you, to be allowed to take part. The public may judge your opinions, but you will never be expelled or condemned for possessing one."

He stared at the impossible woman in consternation.

Many of her points were true. Although she went about her business in ways completely antithetical to his own mores and values, he could not deny that she wanted the same things he did. Fairness. Justice. Equality. A better life for all.

It was easy for him to champion such causes however he pleased, yet all but impossible for her.

"I don't mind disguising myself for investigative missions," she said softly, "although I wish I did not have to don an equally false evening costume in order to be deemed acceptable by society."

He stepped forward.

"I don't expect to change your mind," she said quickly. "My actions will never be seen as those of a 'proper' young lady, nor will my name ever be spoken in Parliament. But I don't need that. What good is a pristine reputation, if I'm the only person it helps?"

"What good is throwing your reputation away if it stops you from helping anyone, including yourself?" he countered. "What do you think will happen if your ruse is discovered?"

"No more soirées," she said with mock relief, "but between now and then—"

"Discovered by a *shopkeeper*," Cole pressed. "Your name in scandal columns will be the least of your problems. You're not an actress on a stage. These are real people. Each time, you endanger yourself physically, legally, and—"

"Legally?" She gaped at him. "Dishonest vendors are the ones who—"

"You are not a magistrate," he reminded her, "or an armed Runner, or a member of the House."

"You're trying to—"

"I'm trying to *protect* you," he burst out. "Can't you see that? I admire where your heart is. I admire that you put the good of the people above yourself. I love that you eschew complaisance in favor of investigation and facts and progress. But I cannot let you—"

"You cannot 'let' me do anything," she spat, "because you do not own me, and you never will. You don't even see the hypocrisy. Men have the freedom to dress in regimentals to risk their lives at war, yet I cannot don a plain bonnet or weigh a bushel of corn?"

"Diana—"

"What would you have me do?" She threw out her hands, her eyes and tone bleak. "Spend the next four decades painting insipid watercolors and fretting over the art of perfect ringlets?"

"I—"

"No," she said dully. "Don't answer. If that's your vision for me, I don't want to know."

She spun away from him and waved a hand toward an oncoming hack.

In one step, he was at her side. "My coach is across the street. Let me take you home."

"You can't," she said, blue eyes accusing. "The Duke of Colehaven alone with frumpy Miss Middleton? What would people think?"

With that, she disappeared into the hack and closed the door.

CHAPTER 11

Diana had never felt less like being at a soirée.

Her spine was pressed against the farthest wall from the dancing, but her mind had never left the Duke of Colehaven. A dozen hours had passed since their confrontation, but her fingers still shook at the memory.

She had been *fortunate* to have been caught by Colehaven and not someone else. For all their impassioned disagreements, he was perhaps the one soul in all of England who would keep her secret without taking action against her.

Diana's spine straightened. Perhaps Thaddeus was the answer. She hated that her unwed state was holding her cousin back from seeking love of his own. But what if they could both have what they wanted?

When Diana had been orphaned, Thad had not hesitated to take her in as her guardian. He also guarded the dowry that Diana's father had set aside for her future husband. When she had first been presented to Society, Thad had denied her request for the money to be transferred to her instead. His duty was to see her married. No further argument allowed.

But that was then. She'd been a debutante, not a spinster. What if Thad could finally be talked into turning over the dowry money?

By ton standards, the nominal sum was pitiably humble. But Diana did not plan to live a lavish life. If she could rent a simple room somewhere out of society's sight, her unconventional behavior would not bring scandal to Thad's name or reputation.

In fact, she could perhaps even become the exact thing she'd been pretending to be: the right hand of a barrister or magistrate who sought to improve England's laws and ability to enforce them.

She grinned in delight. Then there wouldn't be anything to unmask. She'd just be a woman, doing her job. Improving her world. *Openly.* Giddy excitement filled her at the image.

"The Duke of Colehaven," boomed the butler from the top of the stairs.

Diana's smile froze in place, but the rest of her body flushed with heat at the sight. Her damnable attraction to Colehaven was not just a matter of wide shoulders in a coat of black superfine, boyish dark locks curling over his forehead, or that magnetic, arrogant stride.

It was the rest of him that hooked her. The *I personally push for reform* and the *I'm trying to protect you.* The tavern he cofounded to create a space for men to be equal. And yes, the searing memory of unforgettable kisses with their bodies locked together.

If she could draw, her journals would be decorated with illustrated likenesses alongside the faithful transcriptions of their most important conversations.

Excluding the moments where physical desire overtook good sense, of course. Some moments were not meant to be written about, but rather to be relived time and again in the privacy of her mind.

She pushed away from the wall and headed toward the refreshment table. A glass of ratafia would give her something to do with her hands other than wish for another chance to sink them into his hair. Their mouths might be at war, but the rest of their bodies were too compatible for comfort.

"I wondered if you'd come."

The low, familiar rumble sent a delicious shiver across Diana's skin. She did not need to turn around to know who had just stepped into the queue behind her.

"What made you think I'd be at this soirée?" she murmured. "There must be a dozen similar parties unfolding at this very moment."

"I feared I was doomed to find out," came the dry response. "This is my seventh stop tonight."

At this, Diana could not help but glance over her shoulder.

His chiseled face was less than an arm's length away. Closer than she'd hoped, but not nearly as close as she desired. The smolder in his hazel eyes indicated he felt much the same.

"You were looking for me?" she stammered inanely. Of course he was looking for her. Why else would he pretend a love of ratafia?

"I didn't like how we left things." His dark gaze was locked on hers.

She swallowed. "What else can there be to say?"

"I thought you should know that I do recognize the need for standardized units. Twenty-seven types of bushel are at least two dozen more varieties than necessary, and you don't want me to start on the situation with gallons."

She stared at him. "You had your coachman ferry you to seven different balls in order to argue with me about standardizing gallons?"

His cheeks colored. "I'm sorry. I know it's not the sort of subject—"

"It's perfect," she admitted before he could fully apologize.

Some women might wish for a knight on a white steed to climb their balcony and steal them away into the sunset. Diana had just longed to be taken seriously. To be seen. To be heard.

"You were the one who pushed through the Weights and Measures Act of 1815?" she asked quietly.

"One of many," he said. "I was not the leader of that committee, but I was the one who brought their attention to information I had compiled, including several unsigned letters from dissatisfied members of the public."

A tiny thread of pride wiggled its way into her heart. He had seen her words, heard her voice, listened to her arguments way back then. They'd been partners for years. They just hadn't realized it yet.

"*Member* of the public," she corrected with a hesitant smile. "At least for a few dozen of those letters."

"*No.*" He stared at her in disbelief.

The back of her neck flushed, and she nodded. "Yes."

He burst out laughing. "If the Lords only knew…"

Diana's chest thumped with excitement. Colehaven was teasing her, but that was the actual plan. Miss Diana Middleton might be powerless and unimportant, but Colehaven commanded influence. He did not need to hide behind anonymous letters. He could bring her ideas to Parliament as if they were his own.

A duke supporting a common person's ideas in the House of Lords would be the highest praise *any* non-nobleman could aspire to, regardless of gender. A public sign of complete faith.

He'd championed her cause once before. The trick would be coaxing him into a permanent partnership of sorts.

"Ratafia?" asked a footman. It was Diana's turn.

She nodded. "Yes, please."

He ladled the spiced, sweet wine and handed her the glass.

"Thank you," she murmured, but the footman's attention was already centered on the next guest in the queue.

Diana took her cue and faded toward the wallpaper. Here, just like in the House of Lords, it was Colehaven who was important and she who was not.

All she cared about were the good works they could put into place for their fellow citizens. If they could be friends—if they could be a *team*—they needn't limit themselves to weights and measures.

She would be honored to devote her time to any law that could use fact-gathering or an analytical mind to put things into perspective and dream up possible solutions.

Diana had long ago resigned herself to a life of hard work with no recognition. Helping an honorable, loyal, stubborn man like Colehaven to achieve greater success would be just as fulfilling.

But, of course, she was placing the cart before the horse. Just because the duke had listened to her opinion in the past did not mean he wished to do so for the rest of his career.

Without looking at her, Colehaven accepted a glass of ratafia and strode off in the direction of his important, popular friends.

Diana hadn't expected different. In fact, she'd

hoped he would not insist on continuing their conversation after they'd reached the end of the ratafia queue. Friendliness that public would cause far more attention and gossip than either of them wished to suffer.

And yet, a tiny part of her wished he didn't care about the whispers. That friendship was friendship, whether it be two lords who ran the *Wicked Duke* and all of England… or the Duke of Colehaven and a nobody orphan like Diana.

Irritated with herself, she downed half her ratafia in a single gulp and turned to head back to her usual shadows.

A snippet of conversation stopped her from going.

"Did you see Colehaven?" one of the stately matrons whispered to another. "If my Agatha can tempt him to sign her dance card again, I think she has a chance."

"Again?" echoed her companion. "When did he dance with Agatha the first time?"

"Last Season," Agatha's mother said proudly. "He stood up with her on two different occasions. She still has the cards bearing his signatures affixed to her vanity."

The companion gave a sad shake of her head. "That was last year. There are new debutantes to contend with. The Lyndon girl's been out all of a fortnight and is already being bandied about as this season's Original. She's niece to the Earl of Fortescue and beautiful in both looks and manners."

"Agatha is everything that is polite and proper," her mother said hotly.

"She has *freckles,*" her companion whispered as though the word itself was contagious. "A duke needn't settle for anything short of perfection. Especially not one as young and handsome as Colehaven. If my Hester were only a wee more biddable..."

Proper. Biddable. Perfect.

Words that never once had been spoken to describe Diana.

She wasn't related to anyone with a title, could in no way improve Colehaven's connections or standings. She was old, outspoken, the opposite of docile...

There was no reason for depressed spirits or hurt feelings, Diana reminded herself. She didn't want him to *waltz* with her. She just needed him to listen to her. Occasionally. Secretly. The rest didn't matter.

Despite how her twisting heart might feel about the thought of him wed to some vapid, portrait-perfect little girl.

She stared down at her glass. No matter how much she tried to deny her feelings, Colehaven was precisely the sort of man she would want, if she could let herself want a man like him. He was friendly, principled, confident...

Too late, she realized she'd wandered not back to the wallflower perch where she belonged, but closer to Colehaven and his peers.

One of the men wiggled his brows. "Have you seen this year's crop?"

Diana did not need to consult her journal to know that he wasn't talking about potatoes. What Adolphus Fernsby lacked in titled connections, he made up for with shameless flirtation. His name was on every dance card… if the bearer possessed a large enough dowry.

Colehaven shook his head. "Too young."

"Well, one oughtn't dally long," Fernsby pointed out. "If they're still around after two or three years, *something* must be wrong. And besides, those who require an heir and a spare need time to perfect their craft, in case the first few are daughters."

A marquess famed for his love of fox-hunting turned to him in horror. "Stricken with a sister *and* a daughter? Surely Fate cannot be so cruel."

"You jest." Fernsby sniffed in pique. "I hope your future wife spawns nothing but girls."

The marquess shivered. "A dreadful curse. Are you certain you're not a gypsy?"

Fernsby harrumphed and stalked away.

From this angle, Diana could not see Colehaven's expression, but the roll of his eyes was evident in the tone of his voice. "Why does he think we require his direction on whom to wed?"

"As if there's any question," the marquess agreed with a sigh. "We know what sort of woman makes a proper duchess. We'll do our duty when it's time, without the pinks of the ton pecking us like mother hens."

"He does make a good hen," Colehaven mused. "I think it's the way his hair sticks up in the back."

"That style is called the 'frightened owl,' not the 'mother hen,'" the marquess scolded him. "Which you would know, if you would just *glance* at the four hundred fashion plates your sister ordered for you—"

Colehaven groaned. "Not you, too. I thought being a duke meant I didn't need to be fashionable. Aren't young ladies supposed to be more interested in my title than how I tie my neckcloth?"

"Oh, is that a neckcloth?" The marquess asked politely. "I thought you'd misplaced this morning's serviette."

"I hope you *are* cursed with nothing but daughters," Colehaven informed him. "Hellions, every one of them."

Diana stared down into her half-empty glass. They were right. No one needed Adolphus Fernsby or anyone else reminding them what sort of woman made an appropriate duchess. She would need to gird her loins for the inevitable day when Colehaven wed the "right" kind of girl.

The worst part was, Diana needed him to follow the prescribed path. In order for Colehaven to do good works, he had to remain respected amongst his peers. His decision-making could not be called into question. A wife with unexpected quirks would attract unnecessary attention and distract from the true goals.

"Speaking of marriage," the marquess said, "I notice Thad's ward is still unwed."

Safe against the wall, Diana inched close enough to see Colehaven's expression.

"I'm working on it," he assured his friend. "Finding the right match takes time."

"You haven't even found any wrong matches," the marquess pointed out. "I haven't seen her in anybody's company but yours."

Colehaven's gaze sharpened. "When was she in my company?"

"When you queued up for that glass of ratafia you haven't even touched." The marquess cocked his head. "It's not like you to take this long to win a wager. The reason you haven't married her off yet isn't because you…"

"*No,*" Colehaven interrupted firmly. "I've always known what kind of wife I need, and she is certainly not—"

His eyes met Diana's.

She was against a wall, almost out of sight, and somehow he had sensed her presence.

Belatedly.

She spun and walked off before he could call out to her and beg the opportunity to explain his words.

There was nothing to explain. He was right.

Every person in this ballroom knew which young ladies were contenders for titled husbands. Diana's name was not on that list.

Colehaven in particular was acutely aware of her many shortcomings in that regard. He was being practical. Practicality was a trait she admired. There was no reason at all for her eyes to prick with heat or her throat to feel swollen and raw. She'd *known* she wasn't suitable.

She just hadn't prepared to hear him say so aloud.

Diana handed her unfinished ratafia to a footman as she exited the ballroom. She turned down the first corridor and pushed through the side doors leading to the enclosed garden.

The sudden blast of bracing air was welcome on her skin. The sky was clear and full of stars, and the shock of cold kept her mind from returning to the ballroom. Up ahead was another party guest who preferred solitude to revelry.

No, not just any guest. This was—

"Are you trying to catch your death?" the Duke of Colehaven demanded, his eyes widening at the sight of her. He clamped a warm hand about her elbow and dragged her behind a manicured hedge.

"It's not that cold," she protested. "Other people are in the garden."

"Other people have coats." He rubbed his hands over her bare arms. "And nobody else is in this garden. Come back to the ballroom."

"So you can win a wager?"

He closed his eyes. "What I wanted…"

"As I told you before, you do not control me." She lifted her chin. "Nor will any man. I *enjoy* being a spinster."

"No one enjoys being a spinster."

"The fallen ones do," she countered at once. "They enjoy their freedoms and a whole lot more."

In fact, every time she saw him, she could not help but wish she had no reputation to protect. Given the freedom to do so, she would kiss him every chance she could. And if she had no reason to bother with good behavior at all... Diana would not mind being very, very bad.

Colehaven curved his hand over her mouth. "Don't let anyone hear you talk like that."

Like who? They were alone in the garden. Stolen moments were not the same as a life of freedom, but even a stolen moment should not be squandered. She pressed the tip of her tongue to his palm.

He dropped his hand at once, his eyes full of warning. "Diana—"

"If I'm not saving my virtue," she said sweetly, "then it's my currency to spend however I wish. Perhaps I'll wager it."

He gripped her arms. "If you dare—"

"Are you a betting man?" she asked, batting wide eyes. Just because she couldn't have him forever didn't mean they should walk away. Not yet. "I wager you can't shut that beautiful mouth for five minutes and prove yourself immune to a fallen spinster."

"I'll take that bet," he snapped. "Not that I need it. You and I aren't—"

"No talking." She placed a finger to his lips and smiled. "And no touching. You, that is. I can do as I please for five minutes. Agreed?"

His eyes flashed like daggers, but his shoulders

gave a laconic shrug, as if to dare her to do her worst.

Diana fully intended to. He liked to pretend he wasn't ruled by his emotions, his desires. She had five minutes to prove otherwise. She doubted she'd need all five, but intended to enjoy every one. Her smile widened.

She let her finger fall from his lips. If the wind was still cold, she didn't feel it at all.

Her pulse raced in anticipation. She drew herself up on her toes until her mouth brushed the spot on his lip that her finger had touched.

"I'm close enough to kiss," she murmured.

Each syllable brought her mouth closer or further from his, as if each word was a kiss, each sentence a promise of lovemaking.

Just as his lips parted, she lowered her feet, breaking the delicious contact. Perhaps she'd kiss him, and perhaps she wouldn't. This was her wager, not his.

She placed her fingertips to the center of his chest, just below his cravat.

He was wearing too many layers for her to feel the beating of his heart, but his heat was almost scalding.

Letting her fingertips trail against him, she began a slow, hip-swinging circle about him, as if lazily perusing a fine steed at Tattersall's.

Not that she'd been to Tattersall's. Tattersall's was for men, just like everything else. Everything except this moment, this wager, these five delectable minutes where *she* held the power.

The muscles of his upper arm twitched beneath her touch, as if forcing himself to stay perfectly still had wound Colehaven tight.

As she circled behind him, Diana allowed herself the luxury of slowing even further, dragging her fingertips inch by inch across the wide expanse of his shoulders.

"I'm not cold now," she whispered against the back of his neck, where his dark hair curled against the snowy white of his cravat. "I'm imagining how it would feel to touch your bare flesh."

He sucked in a tiny, audible breath.

Diana trailed a finger down his spine. She'd phrased her teasing statement so that it was unclear if she'd never touched a man, or if she lamented being unable to add him to her list. Let him stew on that for the rest of his life, while he was wed to Miss Perfect.

Just as her finger dipped below his waist, she changed course and continued her slow circle around his other side, until her finger caught against the button of his fall.

His muscles tightened visibly. From this angle, he could see her, and his eyes dared her to continue her dangerous game.

She circled the button with her fingertip. The angle of his fall shifted. Colehaven might be holding himself as still as possible, but there was no hiding his arousal.

"I want to touch it," she whispered.

A small groan escaped his throat.

"But I'm not going to," she continued. "If we

touch, we touch each other. We're equals, or we're nothing."

He tilted his hips toward her palm as though to ask, *does* this *feel like nothing?*

"Whatever freedoms you think you enjoy as an unwed gentleman, *I* enjoy as an unfettered spinster. What I do with my time and my body is my business." She ran her fingernails up his chest and lifted her parted lips to his. "I'll share them when and how I see fit."

The heat from his gaze melted her to her core.

She brushed her mouth against his. "Five minutes are up."

"Thank God," he snarled, and swung her against the closest tree.

Before she could so much as gasp, his hands were in her hair and his mouth slanted over hers.

This was no tepid, timid kiss between strangers. This was a claiming, raw and possessive. A demand for surrender.

She would not give it to him. She knotted her fingers in his hair and returned his kiss, passion for passion. Every lick, every nibble, every taste was a dance of fire, marking territory and losing ground as each grasp for control brought each of them closer to the precipice of surrender.

"I'm not yours," she gasped between kisses.

He splayed his hands against her ribs, the pads of his thumbs rubbing indecently against the bottom of her bosom. "Right now, you are."

"Careful," she whispered, lowering one of her

palms dangerously close to his tented fall. "If I'm yours, that makes you mine."

"Then take what you want," he growled. "I'll do the same."

His fingers cupped her breasts as he covered her mouth with his.

Pleasure emanated through her as he expertly teased her nipples. Pleasure, and an exquisite, torturous pressure building between her legs.

Intoxicated, she reached for his fall and thrilled to feel his hard heat pulse against her fingers. What would happen if she—

Music spilled into the garden.

"Are you *mad?*" giggled a female voice. "It's freezing out here. Let's go back to the ballroom."

Diana and Colehaven jerked their hands off each other's bodies.

"You bewitched me," he whispered.

"You make me stupid," she countered.

"Equals," he muttered, and wrapped his arms about her to cradle her to his chest.

His heart was beating just as rapidly as hers.

After a moment, he curved his hands about her arms and gently pulled her upright.

"*Go,*" he commanded. "Whilst some presence of mind still remains."

She frowned. "What are you—"

"I need another moment or twelve out in the cold," he said wryly. "*You* have a guardian who might be turning this residence upside-down in search of you."

"Eep." The cold suddenly rushed back into her bones. "You're right."

With one final glance over her shoulder, Diana fled back inside the house before anyone else could stumble upon them.

The wager had seemed such a good idea. An opportunity to prove to Colehaven that he was neither as perfect nor as immune as he believed. And, if Diana was honest, a chance to circumvent the hypocrisy that let men be rakes whilst spinsters were meant to stay demure and sexless.

But she wasn't certain that either one of them had won the wager after all. Rather than snuff the sparks between them, the night had all but caught fire. Next time…

Diana shook her head. There wouldn't be a next time. They had both learned their lesson. They would keep their hands to themselves from this moment on.

Probably.

CHAPTER 12

When Cole had denied any interest in a woman like Diana, the words had been automatic because they'd always been true. He knew what kind of duchess was expected of him. After spending so many years trying to prove himself, Cole would settle for no less than perfection in a wife.

That Diana had overheard him say so… Well, that hadn't been ideal, but nor had it been untruthful. She would have expected no less.

Except, when his eyes met hers, it was his own tongue that had felt strange forming the words. As if they were no longer true, and the person he was being most dishonest with was himself.

Perhaps that was why he'd just directed his coachman to the Middleton town house. After a brief detour, to prepare a small gift.

Cole strode up the front walk and rapped smartly upon the knocker.

He wasn't thinking *marriage,* of course. But he

also was not *not* thinking marriage. After last night.. He'd felt her nipples between his fingers, for God's sake.

His body tightened every time the memory flashed before his eyes. As it had approximately every five minutes since fleeing the garden.

Five minutes. He'd never be able to hear those words again without reliving Diana Middleton sliding her fingers against his—

"Your Grace," said the butler. "A pleasure to see you. I'm afraid master Middleton is still abed."

"I'm here for the other one," Cole said. The woman he suspected was the real master in this house.

He thought he'd entered into a game of chess, only to discover she'd begun the match years ago and had always been several moves ahead.

"Act of 1815," Cole muttered beneath his breath. "Minx."

The butler's eyes widened. "Excuse me, Your Grace?"

Cole affected a placid smile. "Miss Middleton, if you please."

"Very well." The butler motioned him to the front parlor. "I'll see if she's receiving."

Cole settled himself on the couch, then sprang to his feet and hurried to a wingback chair. When it came to Miss Middleton, he did not trust himself anywhere near a couch. Even if she swept into the room dressed in a mobcap and apron.

She entered wearing a gown of dusky rose with white-striped gauze, and her blond hair was pinned in soft, golden loops. She had never looked more stunning.

And her maid… was nowhere to be seen.

"Where's your chaperone?" he demanded.

She batted her eyelashes innocently. "Do we need one?"

"We need seven or eight," he said. "At this point, iron manacles wouldn't hurt."

The corner of her mouth twitched. "We'll have to settle for Betty."

She tugged a bell pull, then perched on the edge of a narrow chair opposite him, also avoiding the couch. "I hope you haven't come to apologize for last night. I quite enjoyed it."

"I'd like to do it again," he said honestly. "But that's a terrible idea. Most likely, so is this." He handed her the package.

"Oof." She settled the heavy cylinder between her thighs. "What is this?"

"A quarter gallon of refined libation," he said with a straight face. "Using the same methodology for liquid measure as the half peck for dry."

"Horrid scamp," she scolded him. "Now I'm more interested in weighing it than unwrapping it."

A maid appeared in the doorway.

"Thank God." Cole motioned her over. "You must chaperone us."

Diana lifted a finger to stall the maid. "But first, fetch me my basket of scales, Betty."

"Wait—what?" Cole stammered, but the chit was already gone.

Diana grinned at him. "She'll be back, don't worry. Besides, I'm rubbish at waiting to open presents."

She pulled the twine off the package and slid the contents from its brown paper wrapping. Her laughing eyes met his. "A miniature beer barrel?"

He attached the tap. "A beer barrel full of—"

"Shh," she scolded. "You'll ruin the surprise."

As she reached for a bell pull, a footman arrived with a small tea tray.

"You are a prince among men," Diana informed the footman, then ignored the kettle in order to pour ale into two of the teacups.

Cole cleared his throat. "I have a plethora of personalized mugs out in the carriage."

She placed a frothy teacup and a small cake upon a saucer and handed the set to Cole.

He accepted the offering.

"If this is meant to dissuade me from taking advantage of handsome dukes in empty gardens, you're doing a terrible job," she warned him.

"Perhaps it's meant to dissuade you from *other* dukes," he suggested. "Has any of those henwits brought you ale he brewed himself?"

"*Your* ale?" she exclaimed in delight. "Fresh from the *Wicked Duke?*"

"Scandalously so," he assured her. "Do feel free to comment upon the flavor balance's obvious superiority to the swill offered in every other tavern."

She lowered her head to the teacup and inhaled deeply. "I hope your kitchen staff took my suggestion on barley."

"You've spoken to my staff? Wait—you've been in my tavern?" He gaped at her in disbelief. "Have you already tried my new beer?"

"It's a fine gift," she assured him. "And exceptional beer. I had not had the pleasure, and am thrilled indeed to rectify that lack."

"Good," he said. "It's the spoonful of sugar to sweeten what I came here to say."

She added another dollop of ale to her teacup. "I'm listening. I promise."

"I do not regret last night," he began.

"Thank heavens." She glanced up. "I would hate to waste such good beer by tossing it in your face."

"*But,*" he pressed on, "I believe honesty is the only policy, so I must be clear about my intentions."

"You haven't any. Neither do I." She took a sip of ale. "I thought we covered this last night."

"That was before your hand was on my—"

"Your basket of scales, ma'am," announced the out-of-breath maid.

"Thank you, Betty." Diana arched a brow toward Cole. "Should she chaperone us for this conversation, or should I let her have a rest in the next room?"

"Have a rest and this shilling" He tossed a coin to the maid. "Whatever you're paid, it isn't enough."

The maid bobbed a curtsy and slipped the coin in a hidden pocket.

"Come barging in if this parlor gets suspiciously quiet," Cole warned her.

"Or don't," Diana suggested as she tossed the girl a matching coin. "Perhaps you'll sleep so deeply, you'll forget this visit entirely by the time my cousin wakes up."

The maid turned back toward Cole with an expectant expression.

It took only a moment to realize what she was waiting for.

"What the…" He sent a disbelieving glance toward Diana. "Is this what you and Thaddeus do all day? Take turns bribing your own servants?"

She didn't glance up from her tiny teacup of beer. "Hmm?"

Cole tossed the maid a half-crown. "*Chaperone us*. I'm a conscienceless scoundrel. Anything could happen."

"He's a duke," Diana mouthed toward her maid.

The chit made an aggravatingly sympathetic expression, then abandoned them to do as they would.

"Impressive," Cole said. "I brought you beer because entering my tavern would ruin your reputation, but I'm starting to fear what spending an hour in this parlor is going to do to mine."

"Mum's the word," she reminded him. "It'll be like it never happened. Now, take off your clothes."

A startled laugh burst from his throat. He held out his hands. "Give me that barrel. Two ounces of ale is clearly more than you can handle."

"A gift's a gift," she said with a chiding wave of her finger. "Why are you really here?"

Because he wished there *was* a way.

He liked her and he wanted her to like him. She brought a fresh perspective to things he thought he knew inside and out. He desired her, and well knew she desired him right back.

Yet he didn't know how to make it something more. Something *she* would agree to.

"Is it true that one out of every four women never marries?" he asked.

At this, she did glance up from her beer in surprise. "I wouldn't cite a number if I wasn't certain of my facts."

"That right there," Cole told her. "That's why I'm here. I *believe* you. You got the numbers from somewhere—"

"Several somewheres," she assured him. "I have at least a dozen journals dedicated to the composition of England's continuously changing population, with sources clearly notated beneath every fact."

She would, he realized. She probably had a journal dedicated to highhanded dukes who gave unsolicited advice and repeatedly stole kisses. He decided not to ask.

"Most girls collect Ackermann's fashion plates," he teased, using a voice as priggish as possible to indicate his deep disappointment at this flaw in her character.

"Like many women," she countered, "I own the complete collections of both Ackermann and *Costumes Parisien*. Research is research."

He blinked. "Then why are you always..."

"Outrageously frumpish?" she asked with a smirk. "How polite of you to point that out."

"I'm helplessly attracted to the outrageously frumpish," he reminded her. "You may recall a certain moment last night, when my fingers—"

"Misdirection," she interrupted as her cheeks flushed a becoming pink. "My freedoms multiply exponentially when I'm all but invisible to the naked eye."

He suspected she'd used the word *naked* to distract him from this line of talk, but her words had sparked a glimmer of an idea.

Obviously he could not court Diana as she *currently* was. The moment her double life was revealed, the scandal would ruin her as well as destroy the reputation he was trying to build in Parliament. But talking her out of conducting her covert investigations would take some time.

Superficially, on the other hand... If Diana knew half as much about fashion as she did weights and measures, she could *look* the part of a duchess within the space of a single afternoon.

Or a single morning. He glanced at the clock upon the mantel. Half past nine. Had he really brought ale to a young lady's doorstep at half past nine in the morning?

"What time will Thaddeus awake?" he asked instead.

"Noon, on occasion." She tilted her head. "Closer to one o'clock, most of the time. Why?"

He rose to his feet. "Summon your coat. We're going shopping."

In fact, this was the perfect time to do so. Like Thaddeus, most of the ton would be fast asleep. They could be to the linen draper and back without anyone the wiser.

All the same, he fetched the maid from the neighboring parlor. He *probably* wouldn't maul Diana Middleton with kisses in the middle of a draper's shop, but chaperonage was never a bad idea.

"Broomall's on Bond Street," he instructed his driver.

He *could* have let the ladies have the forward-facing seat while he rode backward, but since no one could see inside the coach—and they were properly chaperoned this time—sitting hip-to-hip for a short mile wasn't bending much of a rule.

"I thought you hated shopping," Diana said once the carriage was underway.

Cole blinked in surprise. "I do hate shopping."

But this was different. It wasn't for *him*. At least, only indirectly. The only way he could remain respectable and keep seeing Diana was to make her equally respectable. Or at least look the part. He didn't face such an outing with dread, but rather with excitement.

How would she look, when clothed in the

latest fashions? Who cared about fashion—how would she look with colorful flourishes, instead of unrelenting gray or dull fabrics that blended with the wallpaper?

Cole belatedly realized Diana must have an entire journal dedicated to the wall-coverings of the members of the ton, in order to disappear into the background everywhere she went.

"What color are the walls in the Riddings' drawing room?" he asked.

"Blue-gray damask coupled with oak wainscoting in the primary parlor, pale green paper flocked with olive in the side parlor." She frowned. "Are we shopping for wallpaper?"

"Never again," he assured her as the coach drew to a stop.

The coachman swung open the door and handed the women out of the carriage.

Cole bounded out behind them.

He didn't know much about fabrics and fripperies, but his sister was always going on about Broomall's, so he imagined that was as good a place as any to start. Endless rows of rolled cloths filled the labyrinthine interior.

A bright-eyed attendant rushed over to greet them.

Alarmed, Cole dropped his head to Diana's ear. "You weren't just here dressed as a measures maid, were you?"

"No consumables in this shop," she whispered back. "My current focus is products sold by wet or dry weight."

They were safe. In relief, Cole handed a card to the attendant. "We'll take anything the lady wants."

The attendant pressed the card to his chest. "*Anything* the lady wants?"

"Anything at all?" Diana echoed, her eyes suspiciously merry.

"Provided it's not grey in color or easily mistaken for wallpaper," Cole amended hurriedly. "Anything attractive and fashionable that the lady wants. Anything attractive and fashionable even if the lady doesn't want it. There are no limits. Just—" He waved his hands in the direction of the rows of fabric. "—perform some magic."

The attendant nodded sagely. "All the fashionable magic that the lady wants."

"In that case…" Diana edged next to the attendant and pointed a gloved finger toward Cole's midsection. "Something to replace that waistcoat, don't you think? And that jacket! Look at the curve on the cutaway hem, and the length of the sleeves. The whole ensemble seems like it came from 1812."

"1812 was a fine year," Cole protested. "We passed the Infant Suitors in Equity Entitled to Stock Act, celebrated the fifth anniversary of the Wicked Duke… and besides, we're not here for *me*."

"Aren't we?" she asked, her blue eyes batting in feigned innocence. "You said 'anything the lady wants,' and what I want is for you to unquestionably be the finest-attired duke that London has ever seen."

Cole shook his head. "None of your trickery, Diana. You know very well what I meant to say."

"Irrelevant." She patted his arm as though to console him. "As a legislator, you must know that what is *said* outranks what is *meant*. I shall fully comply with the letter of the law and spend your money exactly how I want, as requested. If you now regret this order, perhaps you will think of it the next time Parliament discusses clarification and simplification of the—"

"Yes, yes," he assured her. "Weights and measures. Loan me your relevant journals when we return to your town house and I will read them. In the meantime, we are not leaving this shop until you have selected enough fabrics to commission a morning gown and an evening gown for every single day of the season."

The attendant looked as though he might swoon on the spot.

"My unmemorable manner of dress is by design," Diana reminded him. "I have more pressing concerns than being picked as a dance partner. I'm not one of those flighty chits with nothing between her ears but embroidered rosebuds and net lace."

"The presence of lace isn't an indisputable sign of vapidity," he pointed out. "Pretty gowns won't stop you from being the cleverest woman in the room."

Vulnerability softened her face. "You think I'm the cleverest woman in the room?"

"You're often the cleverest *person* in the room." He let her see the honesty in his gaze. "If you think fashionable clothing blinds others to that truth, then ostrich feathers and seed pearls are no less as powerful a disguise as mud-brown muslin."

Eyes narrowed in thought, Diana touched a finger to her chin as if scouring a chessboard for the best path to counter a checkmate.

"Very well," she said as if today's visit had been her idea. "So long as for every gown I select for myself, we also commission something new for you."

A handful of women draped in measuring tape and armed with pins and shears materialized out of nowhere.

Cole took a step back. "Gentleman do not require all-new attire twice a day for the length of the season. Buckskins were chosen for their durability precisely because they will be reused time and again. Gossips don't whisper if a man wears the same cravat twice in one week."

She folded her arms beneath her breasts and waited.

"For the love of…" He raked a hand through his hair. "You're just like my sister."

Diana arched a brow. "You don't like your sister?"

"I love my sister!" Cole snapped, only to immediately regret his outburst when the obvious implication blanketed the shop in awkward silence.

He quickly changed direction, all but tripping over the words. "As many gowns as can possibly be made for the lady, and… a dozen jackets and waistcoats for me. No further discussion."

Although this result was not the one-to-one ratio she had cheekily demanded, the smug twinkle in Diana's eye indicated she counted herself the victor of today's battle of wills.

Cole tended to agree.

Parliament could do much worse than have a force of nature like Diana Middleton leading its committees. Come to think of it, Diana could do much more than run circles about the House of Lords. If she put her mind to it, she could become a grand society dame on par with Lady Jersey without blinking an eye.

In fact, that was how he'd explain today's expenditure to Thaddeus. He wanted his ward wed, did he not? Cole was facilitating the process. Not by transforming Diana into someone else, but by revealing her as the strong, capable, beautiful, indomitable woman she already was. The next time she stepped into a ballroom, *no one* would overlook her.

The image stole his breath away as he watched the seamstresses coo over Diana's choices in fabric. Her apparent encyclopedic knowledge of fashion and design had them falling over each other to present the best materials and debate the latest elements *à la mode* in Paris.

"You will be this year's Original," one of the seamstresses gushed.

Diana gave a doubtful shake of her head. "I'm seven years too long on the shelf to become society's darling, I'm afraid."

But was she?

Cole had no doubt Diana knew as much about society and the players within it as she knew about Rumford corn gallons and the proper gauze overlay for figured muslin. Had he believed she would not be able to cope with the role of duchess? Overnight, Diana would make centuries of previous duchesses look like novices.

Felicity currently managed their homes, but of course would not be there forever. While nothing could replace his sister, Cole was certain Diana would make quick work of taking over a household. In fact, hadn't Thaddeus said that Diana's first act upon becoming his ward had been to reorganize his home in order to maximize efficiency?

Cole could not imagine a more Diana-ish reaction.

As for her secret life... what if it didn't have to be secret? The Duchess of Colehaven would command more deference than the mousy under-secretary of an imaginary barrister. Perhaps they could even go on such missions together.

Not that they'd need to do so for long. Cole had successfully pushed weights and measures reform once before. He had no doubt he could do so again. Perhaps not the exact way Diana envisioned, but their aims were the same. Improving the everyday lives of fellow citizens.

"And now Your Grace," said the attendant, sweeping toward Cole with reams of fabric in his hands.

Cole stared at him. "How can you possibly be done selecting every button and material necessary for a complete season's worth of gowns?"

The attendant's eyes widened with awe. "Your friend is remarkably efficient."

CHAPTER 13

Friend. That was how the shopkeeper had referred to Cole's relationship with Diana.

Cole supposed it was true enough. But it was far from all he wanted.

When he dropped Diana back at her town house, he invited her to dine at his ducal residence later that evening. Cole's sister—and an army of servants—would be there to play chaperone, but he encouraged her to bring her cousin and as many maids as she pleased all the same.

He wanted to do this right.

But there was the small matter of a certain wager to dispense with first. He left a note for Thaddeus to call upon him at his earliest convenience, then directed his driver straight to the Wicked Duke.

"Colehaven!" came the familiar chorus as he stepped in from the cold. Clinking glasses and smiling faces surrounded him.

He made his way to his usual spot alongside Eastleigh.

"I resign from the wager," Cole announced.

"You can't resign from a wager," Eastleigh admonished him.

"He can lose, though!" someone else called out.

Laughter mixed with the sound of clinking glasses.

"He can't have *lost*," Eastleigh said.

"Because of his winning streak?" someone asked.

"Ten years isn't forever," someone else agreed.

"You have until the end of the season," Eastleigh said in surprise. "I have never witnessed you giving up, much less four months early."

"This isn't surrender," Cole assured him. "This is the eve of battle."

As skilled a chess player as Diana might be, he doubted she anticipated his next move. But if Cole was in, he was *in*. He would convince her their union was the best possible future.

"Fetch me the betting book," Eastleigh called out, then lowered his voice toward Cole. "Does Thad know?"

Cole shook his head. "I've requested an audience this afternoon."

Something in his voice or face must have caused suspicion, because Eastleigh's green eyes narrowed.

"Does the *lady* know?" he asked dryly.

"I'm not certain she suspects," Cole admitted. "But I owe her both honesty and respect. I cannot ask for her hand whilst my friends all have money riding on the outcome."

"Many gentlemen would," Eastleigh said as the betting book passed from hand to hand in his direction.

Cole shook his head. "Then they're not gentlemen."

If Diana rejected his suit, Cole would get no pleasure from marrying her off to someone else. Winning the bet was worthless if it meant losing Diana. If tonight didn't go as he hoped… then Cole was about to lose both.

He gripped the edges of his chair with suddenly clammy hands. What was he going to do if Diana didn't return his affection?

Eastleigh opened the betting book and accepted pen and ink from a barmaid. With a flourish, the duke wrote the date and *formally concedes loss* below the entry, then handed Cole the pen.

"Last chance," Eastleigh said softly. "If you sign, it's done."

Cole placed the nib to the paper.

CHAPTER 14

"That was the best Banbury cake I've ever had," Diana said as she placed her folded napkin beside her empty plate.

For some reason, her cousin Thaddeus had declined to join her in accepting Colehaven's supper invitation. Diana wasn't certain she had ever heard Thaddeus decline a social occasion before, but of course the timing had been short notice. Thad was no doubt promised to too many other events to count.

"I'm glad you liked it." Felicity Sutton sent a mischievous glance toward her brother. "Banbury cakes are one of Cole's favorites. Had you turned up your nose, he likely would have tossed you out on the street."

"A gentleman does not 'toss' ladies," Colehaven informed his sister firmly. "He gently deposits them out in the cold to fend for themselves."

"I'm glad I passed the test," Diana said with a grin.

Perhaps it was for the best that Thaddeus had been too busy to join them. Diana was fairly certain she'd just consumed his portion.

"With Cole, nothing is as simple as a *test*." Lady Felicity gave a conspiratorial roll of her eyes. "He thinks life is a game of chess."

Excitement filled her as Diana turned toward Colehaven.

"You *do* play," she said, shaking a finger in mock accusation.

He grinned back at her. "Was there ever any doubt?"

"Not you, too," Lady Felicity groaned. "Go start your game. I'll pop in just as soon as I finish... er... rethreading every button in the house. Or counting each ash in the fire. Or anything else that keeps me from repeatedly losing in less than ten moves."

Diana raised an amused brow toward Colehaven. "Queen to H4?"

"Queen to H4," he confirmed sadly.

"Noo." Lady Felicity pushed to her feet. "I refuse to sit still while such nonsensical syllables are bandied about in my presence. Find me when you're ready to discuss phaetons and brandy like normal people."

"Normal debutantes don't know the difference between a puckered hammercloth and a full-plaited hammercloth," Colehaven remarked to his sister's retreating back.

"I'm a spinster, not a debutante," Felicity's voice called from the corridor. "And why would you get into a carriage if you didn't understand how it worked?"

Diana's smile faltered when something in Colehaven's face made her think the "spinster" remark had hit too close to home.

"Are you worried about your sister?" she asked.

His beseeching expression pierced her. "Four-and-twenty isn't *spinsterhood,* is it?"

"It's past 'debutante,'" Diana hedged. "It's also not the end of the world. Look at me, for example."

Colehaven's gaze deepened in intensity. He had rarely ceased looking at Diana from the moment she alighted from her carriage. She swallowed.

"Where's this infamous chess set?" she asked, hoping to deflect attention from the flush of her skin.

He held out a hand to help her to her feet. "This way."

The private drawing room he led her to appeared to be designed with chess in mind. There were books along the walls, a buffet with wine and glasses, and even a small spinet in one corner, but the star of the room were exquisitely carved ebony and boxwood pieces on a mahogany board centered right below the crystal chandelier.

Diana's heart skipped. She hurried forward for a better look.

"I'm almost afraid to touch something so beautiful," she said in awe.

Colehaven's gaze heated. "A familiar sensation."

She blushed and ran a finger against the edge of the fluted table. "Black or white?"

He held out his palm. "Ladies first."

She sat before her sixteen boxwood pieces, hesitant to move one and displace the board's artistic perfection.

"What are you lords up to in Parliament this year?" she asked.

Colehaven's wicked grin curled her toes. "Hoping to distract me with politics? I could discuss the Sikes' Hydrometer Act in my sleep."

"Discuss away," she said as she opened with king's pawn. "I find nothing more enjoyable than strong spirits."

"Except weights and measures?" he asked dryly.

"I shiver at your every word," she told him. "It's like you're speaking poetry."

He met her pawn with his. "Most of us are on several committees at once. I'm hoping to make more progress with the National Debt."

She grinned as she moved a boxwood pawn. "Stop allowing spendthrifts to make the budget?"

"If only it were that simple." His fingers touched his pawn. "It's not that the government should spend less money. It's that we need to spend it more efficiently."

"I have suggestions," she said at once. "Whole journals full of them."

He captured her pawn with his. "I imagine you love to debate as much as you love chess."

"I've had less practice with debate," she admitted as she slid her bishop. "Thad suffers through games with me, but he isn't a lord. My knowledge of current issues comes from the papers. Half the time, we don't hear about laws until they're already enacted."

"We could change that," Colehaven offered as his queen flew. "To my surprise, I quite enjoy arguing with you."

"I wish I could attend the galleries," she said wistfully. Her king side-stepped. "Women used to be admitted. Why did men take the privilege away?"

"It's shortsighted," he agreed with a sigh. "I wish I made the rules."

She burst out laughing. "You literally create the laws that govern the entire country. If that's not 'making the rules...'"

He flashed an impish grin and moved a pawn. "Fair enough. I'll see what I can do."

Diana was not looking at the board, but at Colehaven. Opening the galleries back up to women was an impossible request. She knew it. He knew it. And yet she had no doubt that, for her, he would try.

It made her want to kiss him again.

Not that she had ever stopped wanting. She'd thought of little else since their breathless moment alone in the garden. Even this morning, when he'd looked so forlorn at the idea of being outfitted with new waistcoats, it had been all she could do not to place her hands to his jaw and raise her lips to his.

When she captured his pawn with her bishop, her fingers trembled. Unlike this morning on Bond Street, tonight they were all alone. She'd failed to bring her cousin or a maid. His staff was conveniently elsewhere. Even Lady Felicity had disappeared on the thinnest of pretexts, leaving them to carry on as they pleased.

If Diana *were* to indulge in a moment of reckless passion with a handsome duke, she could scarcely ask for more favorable circumstances.

She glanced up through lowered lashes. Was he thinking the same thing she was?

An unfamiliar tremor threaded her voice when she ventured, "Your Grace?"

"Good God." He reared back as though she had slapped him. "Never say *that* again. I'm Colehaven to most, and Cole to my friends."

Emboldened, she licked her lips and tilted her bosom closer. "Are we just… friends?"

Contrary to her dreams, he did not silence this saucy question by slanting his mouth over hers and making love to her right there on the chess table.

"Would you rather… be a duchess?" he asked instead.

It was Diana's turn to rear back in horror.

"What?" She spluttered. "No!"

"I'm doing this all wrong," he said, and turned

as though to slide from his chair and sink to one knee.

Diana leaped to her feet and all but forcibly held him in place.

"Don't do it," she implored him. "Don't ruin it."

"I'm trying to make it better," he said, his earnest voice and hesitant smile breaking her heart. "We had a moment. I'd like to make it permanent."

She curved her hands about his shoulders and looked straight into his eyes.

"I'm not going to marry you or any man," she said. "I told you. I thought you were listening."

"I hadn't proposed to you myself when you said that," he reminded her, as if no woman alive had ever turned down a duke.

Perhaps Diana really was the first.

"Back then, we were talking speculatively," he continued, his gaze urgent and heartfelt. "You marrying a stranger at some future date. Of course you would be concerned about compatibility. Anyone would. I was, too."

Diana closed her eyes, as if doing so would block out his voice.

It didn't work.

"I think we've proven our compatibility. Mentally and physically." His low voice washed over her like a warm breeze.

She shivered anyway.

One of his hands caressed hers.

"Plus," he murmured as if an afterthought, "it's

a truly splendid duchy. And our cat just had kittens."

When she opened her eyes to face him anew, her voice came out much harsher than she intended. "I do not care about your duchy."

This was only partly true. Now that she knew they existed, she could not help but be intrigued by the kittens.

"I won't marry," she said softly. "Gaining a hundred dukedoms would not be worth the loss of my freedom. You're a good man, but you would *own* me. If you should decide I could no longer keep journals or conduct investigations—"

"Of course you will no longer gad about in working-woman disguises," he said firmly.

She let go of his shoulders and tried not to scream.

This. This was why she could never wed. She loved him, but if he did this to her, she would quickly come to hate him. Whatever compatibility they'd once shared would vanish like a—

Diana groaned and sat down hard in her seat. She loved him, and she still couldn't have him. Without her noticing, he'd managed to corner her on the *real* board. The one where dukes were kings and spinsters were pawns.

Check, but not checkmate. She had a few moves left.

"I'm saying no," she said quietly, "not to choose a life of spinsterhood over a life with you. That is what I'd always planned to do, what I've always believed would bring me joy. But joy is the last thing I feel when I decline the offer to be your duchess."

He did not hide the hurt in his gaze. "Then why decline?"

"It's the wrong offer," she said simply. "I would marry *you,* but you don't want to marry *me.*"

He frowned in confusion. "I just said—"

"You want to change me," she interrupted. "You want to fix me, mold me, marry a different version of me than the woman I am. I don't *want* to stop being me. I don't even think I could. So, no, I shan't marry you. I'd bring scandal and embarrassment to your name, and ruin everything you've tried to build. Both of us would be worse together than apart."

His shoulders tightened. "I disagree. Life is worse when we're apart."

"There is a way," she agreed slowly, as a solution glimmered in the back of her mind.

She desired him, wanted to *be* with him, but refused to be owned by him. Which meant they could never have forever. He would marry someday. She would not. But between now and then… there was no reason to deny themselves what they both desired: each other.

This time, when she rose to her feet, it was not to shake him by the shoulders but rather to settle herself on his lap.

"What are you…" he mumbled, even as his arms circled round to embrace her.

She lowered her mouth to the corner of his

and gave it a feathery kiss. "We needn't bother with marriage to reap the best benefits."

"But..." he said between kisses. "If you don't want to be my wife..."

"I can still be your mistress," she finished, and touched the tip of her tongue to his.

"What?" he stammered against her lips, pulling back to stare at her without understanding. "Instead of a lifetime of marriage, you prefer a life as a mistress?"

She gave a lopsided smile. "I can be a temporary mistress if it makes you feel better."

"It does not," he said firmly.

"It could." She pressed her lips to the corner of his mouth. "One year."

"Diana... No... I want more than a mistress."

She licked his lower lip. "One month."

"I... You..." He kissed her as if he could not bear another moment without their bodies entwined, then jerked his head away gasping for air. "This is the opposite of haggling. You keep removing what I want—"

"One night." She slid a finger beneath the hem of her bodice and gave a saucy tug. "Tonight."

A few hours to do as they would. As they *wished*. To create as many memories as possible. To give into temptation... and to each other.

"Right here? Right now?" His voice was gravelly and tortured. He lowered his lips to the pulse point at the base of her neck, then glanced up, his gaze dark with desire. "This is not how most failed marriage proposals end."

"One seduction." She wrapped her arms about his neck and wriggled against his lap. "I dare you."

He lifted her in his arms and pushed to his feet.

"Gentlemen don't toss young ladies out in the street," she whispered to him.

"I'm far from finished with you," he growled as he strode toward the open door.

Rather than carry her out of his private parlor, Colehaven shut the door, engaged the lock, and stalked toward the fireplace.

"What are you doing?" she asked as he tossed her atop a plush chaise longue.

"One seduction." He climbed on top and slanted his mouth over hers. "You dared me."

A thrill raced through her.

"Me seducing you," she clarified as he tugged his cravat from his neck and tossed it aside. "Not… whatever you're planning to do to me."

"*Everything*." His slow, sensual smile was nothing but wicked promise.

Diana wished she had a neckcloth of her own to dramatically fling aside. A co-seduction was the most magnificent idea she had ever heard.

"Let the games begin," she murmured and pulled him to her.

These kisses were different than before. Less possessive, more arrogant and teasing. As if he knew as well as she did that one night of seduction would never be enough.

Colehaven threaded his fingers with hers, trapping her hands on either side of her head.

He needn't have worried. With every pulse of her heart, with every catch in her breath, her body was declaring itself his to plunder however he pleased. Already the familiar pressure was building within her.

When he broke the kiss at last, she parted her lips to protest. Before she could do so, his mouth began a series of slow, sensual kisses underneath her jaw, along the curve of her neck, down the hem of her bodice.

All thoughts of complaint vanished from her mind. When his mouth at last found her breast, a strangled gasp escaped her throat as she arched into him.

She would not think about tomorrow. Once he realized he needed to find a proper wife—or once her double life was revealed, rendering her fully unmarriageable—they would never have a moment like this again.

But for as long as she could, for as long as they both dared, she would give in to vulnerability and share as many moments of pleasure as they could. She wrapped her legs about him and pulled him close.

For tonight, at least, he was hers.

She opened her gown to him, her body, her heart. This was not the moment to hide her true feelings. This was the moment to take everything within her grasp. To offer the same to him. A chance to indulge their desire, even if they did not admit openly that it meant so much more.

He explored her with his hands, his mouth,

leaving no curve unkissed, no naked skin uncaressed. She was his and he knew it. The seduction worked both ways. Her body responded as if it had been set aflame. As if joining with him was the only hope to quench this insatiable desire.

When his head disappeared between her legs, she lost all grasp of reason altogether. There was no choice but to give herself wholly to the moment, to the man whose soft hair she clutched in her fingers as he worked magic she hadn't known existed.

Her breath still hadn't calmed, perhaps would never calm again, when he fitted himself above her in a way that promised even greater pleasures than the one he had just shown her.

"You're certain you want this?" he murmured against the shell of her ear.

"I've been certain for ages," she confessed boldly as she angled her hips to give him better access. "The only thing I was unsure of was whether we'd have an opportunity."

"We can have as many opportunities as you like," he promised.

She doubted that was true, but it didn't matter. Nothing mattered except for the glorious fullness, hot and hard and slick, joining their bodies together. A flash of pain, and then only pleasure as he gave her his body and his caresses and his kisses all at once.

He was not making love to her as if there would be a thousand other opportunities. He was holding nothing back at all, not his desire, not his heart. They were joined together in every way that mattered, body and soul, eye-to-eye, kiss to kiss, as if this moment was all they would ever have. As if there was no choice but to give everything while it was still theirs to give.

For her, there had never been a choice. Her body belonged to him.

Even if she never could.

CHAPTER 15

When Cole awoke, he did not reach out in search of Diana. She was not in his bed. Not yet.

She had returned home shortly after love-making the night before, not wishing to stay away so late as to arouse her guardian's suspicion.

Unnecessary, since Cole fully intended to secure Thad's permission to ask for his ward's hand. Besides, returning an hour or two after supper still made for a far earlier night than attending any given society event.

Granted, Diana had not formally *accepted* Cole's proposal. Not with words. But she had trusted him with her body. Allowed him to claim her virginity. In the eyes of society, she was ruined. There was no choice but to marry Cole.

Admittedly a less romantic outcome than the immediate and enthusiastic "Yes!" he'd been hoping for, but at this point any "yes" would do.

Whatever doubts Diana held, Cole had none

whatsoever. She would be a splendid duchess. Clever, compassionate, tenacious. They would make a marvelous team. Cole could scarcely wait. Three weeks of banns would feel like a lifetime.

But first, a gentleman was required to make things official.

He dressed and broke his fast and spent the morn preparing for tonight's first parliamentary meeting for as long as he could, then set out for the Middleton household.

If Thaddeus was still asleep at half twelve, Cole would drag the man out of bed himself. There was a contract to arrange, a wedding to plan, a new life just around the corner.

When the butler answered the door, Cole greeted him with a smile. "A wonderful day to you, Shaw. Is the master at home?"

"I believe he's expecting you, Your Grace." Shaw led Cole not to the guest parlor, but to Middleton's private sitting room.

The last bubbles of nervousness disappeared from Cole's belly. This was a good sign. An excellent sign. Thaddeus had roused himself at the crack of noon in order to sign the wedding contract.

Cole would leave the question of banns or license up to Diana, but the moment the vows were spoken, he and his new bride would finally be able to—

"Why are you here?"

He spun around, heart pounding uncertainly. The voice hadn't belonged to Thaddeus, but rather to Diana. And she had not sounded pleased to see him.

She stood just outside the doorway with a dubious expression.

His future duchess was not wearing one a fashionable gown, nor was she half-hidden beneath a dingy mobcap and a maid's apron. She had retreated to her wallflower disguise. Her arms were folded beneath her bosom and her ice-blue eyes sparked with fire.

"Performing the next step," he replied at once. "You value efficiency, so I doubted you'd wish for me to dawdle. How did you sleep? I missed you when—"

"Do you *ever* listen to me?" she burst out. "I said no."

"Yes," he agreed, frowning. "And then we removed our clothes and performed an act reserved for husbands and wives—"

"—or whores and dockworkers, or courtesans and lords, or spinsters and whomever they bloody well fancy."

He blinked. "I'm actually not certain that's how that works. At least not for respectable spinsters. Any young lady, married or not, who hopes to maintain a proper reputation—"

"When have I ever been proper?" she demanded. "Or showed any inclination to stay in the tiny box society has painted for me? Name *one* time I was exactly like all your proper young ladies."

"I..."

"You don't want *me*," she said. "You want *your* vision, your limitations, your terms. You want a Diana-shaped marionette that will simper on cue and never risk her precious voucher to Almack's."

His muscles tightened. "That's not fair."

"To either of us," she agreed, eyes flashing. "You have the right to marry a perfect little doll. Go find her. As long as I'm unwed, I have the opportunity to live as *I* please."

"I would never—"

"You already have." Her voice was hollow. "You still do. That's the problem. I will not give up my principles or my battles, and you won't accept me with them. We can't have each other. Not like that."

He shook his head in confusion. "But you let me..."

"I didn't let you do anything," she said through clenched teeth. "Last night was both of us, deciding together. If you can't see the difference..." Her fingers shook. "It would be better if you weren't still here when my cousin comes downstairs. Goodbye, Cole."

She moved aside, leaving no doubt that she wished for him to leave with as much alacrity and efficiency as he'd demonstrated in his unsolicited visit.

Cole inclined his head, and did as she wished.

There was no point in arguing. This time, her unequivocal *no* had been more than clear. Even to a pining fool like him.

He returned to his carriage, but not to his

town house. He wasn't ready for the permanence of its unwelcome emptiness yet.

Instead, he bid his coachman drive him to the Palace of Westminster. Parliament wouldn't open its first session for three more hours, which would hopefully give Cole enough time to push his failed marriage proposal out of his mind and focus on the speech he was meant to give to his peers on public works and fisheries.

Tonight would determine his place for the rest of the parliamentary season.

This was his one chance to make the right impression. If he appeared knowledgeable enough, reliable enough, *lordly* enough, they might choose him to replace Fortescue as committee leader.

It was what he wanted. What he had been working toward. And, if he were as honest as Diana, it was a goal far easier to achieve without her.

They wouldn't trust him with Acts of Parliament if he couldn't make his own wife respect society's rules. And he certainly couldn't leap on stage blathering about an overabundance of bushels or why England should ape Napoleon's meters. Not without becoming a laughingstock, an object of ridicule, never to be trusted again.

And yet her words still stung his ears. *Have you* ever *listened to me?*

CHAPTER 16

"What are you doing back here?"

Diana lifted her unfocused gaze from the floor outside her cousin's private drawing room to find him at the other end of the short corridor.

Normally at this hour, Thad's hair was still mussed from his pillow, his brown eyes still blurry with sleep. Today he looked as though he had been up for hours. His cheeks were ruddy as if from wind and a pair of riding gloves dangled from one hand.

More unusual, his dark eyes were not vacant and sleepy, but bright and alert and narrowing with concern. His long stride brought him to her side in seconds.

"What is it?" He pried her shoulders from the wall and led her to a leather chair in his study. "Tell me what's happened."

Diana tilted the back of her head against the chair and squeezed her eyes tight.

What happened had nothing to do with Thaddeus. What she intended to do—or not do—with her future affected her cousin very much.

He had taken every possible step to give her the best chance on the marriage mart. Dragged her to every possible beau monde soirée, even roped a duke into the impossible mission of marrying off his ward.

Diana had spent the past five years thwarting her cousin's efforts. She'd been afraid if she told him the truth—that she never planned to take a husband—that her presence would no longer be welcome.

Thaddeus had agreed to be his orphaned cousin's temporary guardian. He had not enlisted himself as permanent provider to a poor relation who chose to remain a dependent spinster on purpose.

She had accused Colehaven of not listening to her, of not recognizing her perspective nor respecting her wishes.

But she hadn't even given her cousin the courtesy of an explanation, preferring to let him try so earnestly to give her opportunities for something she didn't even want, rather than be brave enough to sit down and tell him the truth.

It was past time.

Diana opened her eyes. "Colehaven asked me to marry him."

"Congratulations, cousin." Thaddeus's shoulders relaxed in obvious relief.

"I declined."

There. The topic was broached. Now he would know just what kind of ward he had.

Thad's brow furrowed. "You dislike Colehaven?"

Diana shook her head. She loved Cole. But it wasn't enough.

"If your sights are set higher than a duke," Thaddeus said slowly, "you should know that only leaves foreign princes and the Regent himself, who I'm afraid is already taken."

Diana dropped her face in her hands. Her cousin was so deuced *kind.* She hated to shatter his good opinion of her.

She forced herself to look up anyway.

"I can't marry him," she said miserably. "Or anyone proper. *I'm* not proper, and I don't intend to change my ways. A duchess is important amongst the ton, but I'd rather be important to everyday people. To make a real difference. I've been slipping out in the mornings, dressed as something I'm not, in order to—"

Diana's halting explanation cut off at the sight of her cousin's face.

He wasn't surprised. *He wasn't surprised.*

He was sitting there patiently, allowing her to tell her story her way, at her own pace. A shocking, scandalous confession that didn't surprise him in the least.

"You *knew?*" she blurted in disbelief. "How long have you known?"

"From the beginning," he said with a nonchalant shrug. "I may not be good at chess, but I'm competent at managing my affairs. At first, that included a new ward. Then my affairs included a ward who purloined aprons from the staff quarters and slunk out the servants' exit. I haven't been bored for a single moment since your arrival."

Heat flooded her cheeks. Of course the servants had seen her. She'd assumed they guarded their tongues, given her position compared to theirs. Instead, her cousin had known the entire time.

"Why didn't you say anything?" she asked.

"Because you didn't," he said simply. "Whenever you were ready to talk, you would. Until then, it was my duty to keep you safe. Since you stubbornly refused to take a maid with you on your excursions—"

"I was anonymous," she protested. "Or trying to be."

"I made certain never to impinge upon your subterfuges," he assured her. "I kept to the shadows and daresay became reasonably adept at disguises of my own."

Someday, Diana might look back on this moment and laugh. Today, she was simply bewildered.

"Why didn't you read me the riot act?" she asked. "You could have locked me in my room, banished me to the countryside, sent me off to a convent or some sort of asylum for incorrigible, ungrateful wards—"

"*Diana.*" Thaddeus took her hands in his.

"You're not my ward. You're an adult woman. Whether I agree with your choices in mobcaps and dukes, this is your home, too. For as long as you want it."

A thick lump filled her throat, preventing any words from escaping. All she could do was give his hands an answering squeeze and blink away the sudden pricks of heat in her eyes.

"I don't want to change you," her cousin said softly. "I just want you to be happy."

The right words, from the wrong man.

Diana's shoulders crumpled. She could have the life she wanted, but not the person she wanted to share it with. And no matter how miserable she felt inside, it would have to be enough.

It was the best she was going to get.

CHAPTER 17

Cole crumpled up the report he'd kept rewriting for the past several hours and tossed the entirety into the fire.

Parliament wouldn't resume until four o'clock this afternoon. Perhaps between now and then, the best use of his time would be to take himself down to the Wicked Duke and drink until he forgot about Diana.

If enough ale existed in the world to make that happen.

"Still moping?"

Cole jerked his head up in time to witness his sister shove an oversized basket into his study and slam the door without waiting for a response.

He hadn't told her what happened with the House of Lords or with Diana, so he couldn't imagine why Felicity suspected him to be moping.

A state difficult to maintain whilst plucking rambunctious kittens from every precarious surface in his study.

Cole leaped up from behind his desk, but it was too late.

The demons had been unleashed.

He looped his arm through the handle of the now-empty basket and began lurching about his study after a swarm of extremely agile kittens.

"I'm shipping you to Australia," he shouted toward the other side of his closed door. "With these dratted kittens!"

"Have to catch them first," came his sister's laughing voice, already almost too faint to hear. She'd be harder to catch than the damn kittens.

The basket was large enough to hold all six of them, but lacked a lid to keep them safely contained.

Whenever Cole did manage to scoop a tiny ball of fur from a priceless painting or a one-of-a-kind globe, the kittens immediately managed to scamper out of the basket and up his cravat, or drag their tiny claws down the sides of his breeches.

When at last he gave up and threw himself upon his settee in exhausted defeat, the kittens joyfully pounced upon his chest and made themselves at home, as if no corner of the ducal residence was quite as comfortable as the lapels of the duke himself.

He ran his fingers over their soft little spines. They purred their approval.

Cole supposed nothing in life was ever completely predictable. Expecting it to be—or trying to force a pattern that didn't exist—was impossible. Even when life didn't go to plan, the detour wasn't necessarily for the worst.

Like the kittens snuggling against the dented folds of his cravat, Diana was lively and unpredictable. Unlike the kittens, he could not keep her caged for her own safety, or his peace of mind.

A wife was not a pet. Regardless of the letter of the law, he had no wish to control her. He wanted their bond to be genuine. He wanted her to *want* to be his duchess. But what exactly was he offering in return?

A cage. A leash. A declawing. Suppression of all the wild, beautiful things that had attracted him to her in the first place.

He'd thought she'd come around to his perspective. They had so much in common. They both knew what it was like to lose everything. To be orphaned, to start anew, to be scared, to triumph anyway. They both wanted to do everything in their power to make their world a better place.

But even if they came from similar backgrounds, even if their hopes for the future were the same, the paths they took to get there needn't be perfect copies of each other.

After tragedy struck, he'd gained a title, a fortune, a voice in Parliament. When Diana was orphaned, she'd lost her home, had her life uprooted, her existence wholly defined by how good a wife she could be for a total stranger.

One of the kittens climbed up the side of

Cole's face and settled against the crevice between his forehead and the settee.

He didn't dislodge her. His mind was not on kittens, but on Diana.

With discomfort, he began to realize that expecting her to drop everything she cared about, to change her very personality in order to play proper duchess for him was, at best, myopic and vain.

Made worse because his motives centered about making life easier for him, when his life was *already* easier.

The entire reason she'd resorted to duplicitous playacting was because openly pursuing her passions wasn't an option.

He bolted upright, to the surprise of several kittens.

Duplicitous was the wrong word. So was "playacting." For Diana, *barrister's secretary* and *measures inspectress* weren't roles to be acted. They were positions she might have filled in another life. Careers she might have enjoyed.

Her covert research-gathering wasn't a disguise. It was the real Diana, doing what she loved, being herself. Courageous enough not to let anything get in her way. Not the world, not her true identity, not even the Duke of Colehaven.

Diana was Diana, and would always be Diana. Chess games and research journals, crusades against injustice and unbridled passion, always on the precipice between impending scandal and political breakthroughs. Breathtakingly beautiful inside and out, and completely impossible.

Either Cole accepted that, accepted her, or he had to set her free. She deserved nothing less.

The question was whether he deserved *her*.

CHAPTER 18

"Do you want to go to a dinner party with me tonight?"

Diana glanced across the tea table at her cousin. "Do I have to?"

He shook his head. "No."

No.

Diana lowered her teacup and gazed back at her cousin.

His face held a hint of sadness, but his eyes were sincere. He wished she would go. Not to get rid of her, but because he enjoyed her company. He liked going to events together. But it was up to her.

That made all the difference.

"All right," she said.

His face lit up.

Diana found herself smiling back.

She would have gone anyway, of course. Until today, she hadn't realized she had a say in the matter. Yes, Thaddeus had been trying to find her a husband. Not because he wished her gone, but because he wished her happy.

Guilt twisted in her stomach. She certainly hadn't gone out of her way to return the favor.

"Maybe I'll wear something distinguishable from the wallpaper tonight," she said with a self-deprecating smile. "Maybe I'll even join the conversation."

He placed both hands to his chest as if in the throes of apoplexy. "Who are you? What have you done with my cousin? And how long can you stay in her place?"

She tossed a serviette at him. "Beast."

He grinned at her unrepentantly. "They're not all bad, you know. Believe it or not, the number of peacock feathers in a woman's hair does not correlate inversely with her intelligence."

Diana wrinkled her nose and sighed. "I have a feeling *I'm* the awful one."

Her cousin was right. Just because the ton was unashamed of its frivolous interests did not mean none of them cared about the plight of the people or the state of current laws.

That was what Cole had been trying to show her when he'd forced her to shop. She *liked* fashion. He knew it. She'd thought if she indulged such fancies, it made her less serious than she wished to seem. Less worthy of being listened to.

But blending with the background erased her voice altogether. Refusing to take an active part in customs she deemed stifling and silly meant turning her back on the very people in the best position to help.

Cole was not a lone swashbuckler, cutting swaths through fusty members of Parliament in a one-man mission to bring cohesive bushel descriptors to the people.

He was not responsible for the Weights and Measures Act of 1815. Neither was she. There was an entire committee, plus the House of Lords and the House of Commons. She and Cole were agents of change, but they could do little without the staunch support of others.

By thinking of the ton as adversaries, she had devoted her energy into "Diana versus Everyone" instead of "Diana and Everyone against Injustice." Cole's world was just as valid as hers.

They just couldn't live in it together. Not if he wasn't willing to bridge the gap with her.

Shaw strode into the room. "Duke of Colehaven to see Miss Middleton."

Thaddeus arched his brows toward Diana. "Should I fetch my pistol or make myself scarce?"

"At ease, cousin," she assured him. "I don't hate Cole. I'm just not going to marry him."

"I'm here to change your mind," came a low voice from the corridor.

Diana and Thaddeus whirled to face Colehaven.

"I left this 'gentleman' in the entryway," Shaw said with a sniff.

"The entryway is three paces from the parlor," Colehaven put in. "I can hear you talking."

"I'll fetch the pistol," Shaw said and strode from the room.

Colehaven crossed directly in front of Diana and dropped to one knee. "Every moment without you is like stars vanishing from the sky. You are the light in the darkness. My compass to—"

Thaddeus leaped to his feet.

"You know, Shaw really oughtn't to be left in charge of a pistol," he said as he edged out of the parlor. "Do carry on without me."

Heart racing, Diana turned back to Colehaven.

"I'm in hell without you," he said baldly, his eyes on hers. "But I have come to realize our future isn't about me. Nor is it about you. Marriage would mean the one thing you begged for us to be: equals."

Diana cocked her head. "Are those scratch marks on your face?"

"Kittens," he said with a wince. "Free to a good home. Now, pay attention."

She folded her hands in her lap and nodded. "Equals, you were saying?"

"Equals." He scooted closer on one knee. "You're right, of course. Men and women aren't equal in the eyes of the law, but—"

She shot up straight. "You can fix that?"

He grimaced. "Meters might be easier."

"True." She let out a long sigh. A woman could dream. "One thing at a time, I suppose."

"Just so." He pressed a finger to her lips. "If I could take the floor for just a moment, you'd see that I'm trying to perform a persuasive romantic soliloquy."

She frowned. "I think 'soliloquies' are when one is talking to oneself. This might be a monologue?"

"Definitely not a monologue," he assured her. "'Mono' means just one speaker, and you haven't stopped interrupting since I began."

Diana mimed sewing her lips closed and motioned for him to continue.

"Everyone deserves love," he said in a rush, as though the invisible thread binding her mouth shut could break at any moment. "And everyone deserves happiness. You were the one who said to me, 'If it can be improved, improve it.' Everything will be improved if we do so together. Our own lives, plus the lives of others, as well as the very concept of what a husband and wife should be: a team."

Hope began to fill Diana with lightness. This did not sound like a man who wanted her to give up her dreams for him. This sounded like a man who wanted to chase their dreams together.

"I don't want to change you," he said softly. "No matter what you might think or what twaddle I might have said. Your contrary, big-hearted nature is the reason I love you."

Diana's eyes widened as her heart fluttered in her chest. She couldn't have interrupted now if she'd tried. He'd stolen her very breath.

"I don't want you to pretend to be like everyone else," he continued. "If I was tempted by 'normal,' I'd have married it by now. I don't want to make do with the status quo. I want *you*. For better and for worse, for bonnet and for mobcap. I want it all."

Her breath tangled in her throat. She had believed for so long that she couldn't have it all. He wasn't just trying to convince her it was possible. He was handing it to her.

"Diana Middleton," he said, his voice solemn and gentle. "I won't ask you to be my wife. Instead, I beg you to take me as your husband."

Her eyes pricked with tears.

"Er, Diana?" he said nervously. "We've concluded the monologue bit. Now is when you give some sign as to whether it worked."

She took a deep breath. "Did you bring beer?"

"It's in the carriage," he replied automatically, then narrowed his eyes. "But you don't get any unless you marry me."

"Checkmate." She launched herself into his arms. "You beautiful, foolish man, I love you more than ten hogsheads of beer and a thousand perfect disguises."

"Thank God," he murmured into her hair as he held her tight. "It also seems I love you more than my own career. I was meant to take the floor last night to discuss public works and fisheries. But as soon as I finished, I launched into an impromptu speech on the importance of simplifying our unnecessarily chaotic system of weights and measurements into unified, manageable units."

She lifted her head in alarm. "You did what?"

"Don't worry," he assured her. "I give credit where credit is due. I heavily cited research from the foremost expert on the topic. Perhaps you've heard of Miss Diana Middleton?"

"You did *what?*" She dug her nails into his shoulders and stared at him with horror. "But that was your chance! Who did they pick for committee leader?"

"Me," he said with an impish grin. "Not of fisheries, but of weights and measures. If only there was someone with years of firsthand knowledge who could join me on my quest to analyze the current climate and work out a proper solution. If you could point me in the direction of a competent inspectress—"

This time, Diana interrupted him not with words, but with a kiss of complete surrender.

EPILOGUE

June 1824
London, England

At half midnight, the black sky above the Palace of Westminster was speckled with stars. The moon's waxing crescent lent its shimmering glow to the rows of gas lights flanking the Westminster Bridge.

The Duke of Colehaven cared about none of this.

He sailed from the palace to his waiting coach without so much as a glance at the night's beauty. The carriage door was scarcely shut before he was urging his driver to fly to Grosvenor Square with all haste. But Cole was not fleeing Parliament. He was racing home to tell his wife the good news.

Diana was not in the nursery or playing with kittens or organizing her notes in her private study. She was bending over a barrel in their brewing room, her journal in one hand and a mug of beer in the other.

She barely had a chance to set down her sloshing ale before Cole swept her off her feet and swung her in mad, giddy circles.

He tried to cover her with kisses, but couldn't stop grinning long enough to make proper work of it. "We did it, darling!"

She grinned back at him. "You managed to pick out a fashionable waistcoat?"

"*Minx.*" He set her down in order to thrust a painstakingly copied sheaf of documents into her hands.

Her eyes lit up even before she glanced at its contents. "This calls for a celebration! Pour yourself a beer, my love."

"There's no time for ale." He flapped his hands toward the papers. "Read, read!"

Diana cleared her throat and affected the pompous, ramrod-straight posture of a court crier. "An Act for ascertaining and establishing Uniformity of Weights and Measures."

It was all Cole could do not to bounce about the brewing room like a mischievous kitten. He consoled himself by downing half of his wife's ale.

"Whereas it is necessary for the Security of Commerce, and for the Good of the Community, that Weights and Measures should be just and uniform…" Diana continued, her posture relaxing and her grin widening with each new word. With a squeal, she dropped the papers upon the brewing table and launched herself back into Cole's arms. "We *did* do it!"

"No grams and meters," he warned her as they spun about the room.

"I'm thrilled with the demise of twenty-seven different kinds of bushels," she assured him, laughing. "You've achieved a miracle. Imagine—one single size for a gallon!"

"I don't have to imagine," he informed her solemnly. "The document I showed you clearly states that a 'gallon' is a standard unit of volume, defined as ten pounds of distilled water weighed in the air at the precise temperature of sixty-two degrees of Fahrenheit's thermometer, with the barometer configured at—"

She pressed her lips to his, sending all thoughts of imperial measures scattering to the wind with the magic of her kiss.

His friends might have teased him for breaking his ten-year winning streak with the loss of the wedding wager, but Cole knew the truth. The passionate embrace of the clever, stubborn, irresistible woman in his arms was worth far more than any bar-room bet. He'd lost nothing but loneliness and won the love of a lifetime.

He'd wager nothing on earth could be better than that.

THE END

~

THANK YOU FOR READING

Love talking books with fellow readers?

Join the ***Historical Romance Book Club*** for prizes, books, and live chats with your favorite romance authors:

Facebook.com/groups/HistRomBookClub

Check out the ***12 Dukes of Christmas*** facebook group for giveaways and exclusive content:

Facebook.com/groups/DukesOfChristmas

Join the ***Rogues to Riches*** facebook group for insider info and first looks at future books in the series:

Facebook.com/groups/RoguesToRiches

Check out the ***Dukes of War*** facebook group for giveaways and exclusive content:

Facebook.com/groups/DukesOfWar

And check out the official website for sneak peeks and more:

www.EricaRidley.com/books

Don't forget your free book!

Sign up at http://ridley.vip for members-only exclusives, including advance notice of pre-orders, as well as contests, giveaways, freebies, and 99¢ deals!

ACKNOWLEDGMENTS

As always, I could not have written this book without the invaluable support of my critique partner, beta readers, and editors. Huge thanks go out to Darcy Burke, Tessa Shapcott, Erica Monroe, and Tracy Emro. You are the best!

Lastly, I want to thank the *Historical Romance Book Club* facebook group and my fabulous street team. Your enthusiasm makes the romance happen.

Thank you so much!

ABOUT THE AUTHOR

Erica Ridley is a *New York Times* and *USA Today* best-selling author of historical romance novels.

In the new *Rogues to Riches* historical romance series, Cinderella stories aren't just for princesses... Sigh-worthy Regency rogues sweep strong-willed young ladies into whirlwind rags-to-riches romance with rollicking adventure.

The popular *Dukes of War* series features roguish peers and dashing war heroes who return from battle only to be thrust into the splendor and madness of Regency England.

When not reading or writing romances, Erica can be found riding camels in Africa, zip-lining through rainforests in Central America, or getting hopelessly lost in the middle of Budapest.

~

Let's be friends! Find Erica on:
www.EricaRidley.com

CPSIA information can be obtained
at www.ICGtesting.com
Printed in the USA
LVHW031012050519
616703LV00001B/433